VINDICATION

League of Vampires

RYE BREWER

VINDICATION

The seventh book in the League of Vampires series brings you more witches, vampires, fae, shades, and sexy characters in swoonworthy romances and nail-biting action.

When revenge is a being's sole purpose in existence, does this soul burning passion for vengeance end after vindication is achieved?

⊙⊙⊙

Cover Art by
www.mirellasantana.deviantart.com

I

JONAH

The difference between Avellane and the human world was stark as Anissa and I stepped through the portal dividing the two.

I blinked hard, still halfway in the realm we'd just left. No wonder Anissa liked it so much here.

"You all right?" she asked with a knowing smile.

"That place..." I shook my head, blowing out a sharp gust of air. "It's beautiful."

"An understatement," she murmured, looking back in the direction of the swirling energy vortex.

Was there longing in her eyes? Yes, but not for the lush landscape or the heavy scent of flowers. She longed for her father's happiness and was hurting on his behalf.

I took her hand. "I'm sorry about Tabitha."

She pressed her lips together hard enough to make them all but disappear. "I can't believe life is this cruel. I just found her again."

"I know." I hoped mine was a reassuring tone. I knew how hard it was, losing her mother again.

The fact was, Gregor's and Felicity's accounts made it

seem fairly clear Tabitha had met a bad end. Anissa was right, and it was something I had known for a long time: life was cruel, especially in our world.

She halted short of entering headquarters, pulling me to a stop along with her. "Promise me something, Jonah."

"Anything. You know that."

She bit her lip, eyes sparkling in the low light coming from the cathedral's many windows.

Sirene had lit the place up a little while we were gone.

"Please, don't squander the chance to patch things up with your father."

I couldn't help my hackles going up a little at the mention of him. "It's not the same situation," I reminded her.

"But it is. It is."

"You're upset, and I understand. But it really isn't the same. He's not my father anymore—or didn't you hear him insist so every time we've been together? He makes it a point to remind us whenever he gets the chance that he's Fane now. Not Dommik. It simply isn't the same."

"But if you had the chance, you wouldn't waste it. Would you?"

I sighed, doing what I could not to roll my eyes too obviously. She was only trying to do her best and fix relationships. It was her nature, much more so than the assassin Marcus had once turned her into. She cared deeply, passionately—sometimes too much.

"No," I admitted, the word wrenching itself from my chest. "I wouldn't waste the chance. But there's a lot more to it."

"It's only I wouldn't want you to ever look back and see the chances you wasted. That's all. I wouldn't wish it on anyone, but especially not somebody I love."

I raised her hand to my lips and planted a gentle kiss on

the backs of her knuckles. "Which is why I love you. You have a good heart. And remember, there's always a chance your mother survived whatever happened in ShadesRealm. Think of at what she's already survived."

I loved Anissa. She was so much more fae than vampire, though I doubted she realized it. She didn't quite have the mercenary ways of my kind, no matter how Marcus had tried to instill them in her.

Her smile was wise, wistful. "I think there's only so many second chances a person can have. You know what I mean? What if my mother used all of hers up?"

I didn't have an answer for that, but she wasn't waiting for one.

"Come on," she whispered, squaring her thin shoulders. "You've got a bunch of vampires to look after."

"Thanks for the reminder." I chuckled wryly in an attempt to add levity to the situation.

As before, the interior of the cathedral was quiet. Too quiet.

"What do I have to do to get these guards working?" I growled, forgetting about the conversation we'd had in favor of the seemingly hopeless situation I was in.

"All's quiet," Anissa reasoned, her voice echoing despite how low she kept it. "That's a good thing, right? We could've come back to World War Three. Let's be grateful for small victories."

I snorted, glancing around. "You're right. I'm too tense."

"Sirene's enchantment is working, too," she pointed out. "Keeping things under control."

That was what bothered me most, and she'd put her finger on it before I could. "Where is she, anyway?" I wondered aloud as we crossed the length of the Great Hall, wandering down the corridor leading to the room in which the guards had been playing cards, among other side rooms.

They were all empty, silent except for a single guard who stood sentry at the back entrance.

"Where's the witch Sirene?" I asked him as I approached, my tone instantly turning clipped and official. They needed to know who was boss, even if it was only in the interim, until a new leader was put in charge of the League of Vampires.

He shrugged. "I saw her once, I remember, but she was busy doing whatever it was she was doing. I haven't seen her since."

How helpful.

Only Anissa's pointed stare at me over his shoulder kept me from pressing harder. I was far too wound up—never, in all the years I had led the Bourke clan, had I taken such a hard stance on those working under me. Not even in the early days immediately after the disappearance of my parents, when I'd been half out of my mind.

"If you see her, let her know I'm looking for her." I turned away before he could get a look at the conflict working its way across my face.

I wanted to berate him, yell out my frustration at the sense that everything was slipping out from between my fingers like sand. I couldn't seem to keep all the plates spinning at once, and it seemed as though my sanity was suffering as a result.

"You have to relax a little," Anissa whispered as we hurried side-by-side down the corridor.

"You're one to talk. I don't think I've ever seen you relax."

"Right, right, and I'm sure I'd be just as tightly wound as you are if I were in your shoes. This has all happened so quickly, and I'm afraid you haven't been able to catch up to it."

"You're probably right." I couldn't remember the last time I'd drawn a deep, full breath.

Maybe back when I proposed to Anissa, when we were alone. Why couldn't we have more time like that? That was what I needed more than anything else.

"Just calm down. Sirene's around here somewhere. This place is huge, after all. The dungeons, maybe? She might have gone down there for the sake of checking on the prisoners, to be sure the enchantment kept the dungeon secure?"

"Could be true." I forced my muscles to relax, realizing how tight my shoulders, neck, and back were.

Nobody respected a leader who led through intimidation —not for very long, at any rate. And anyone in the position to guard the cathedral labored under a rather violent, threatening leader for decades before I came on the scene. They were immune to me after having lived through Lucian for so long.

With this in mind, I was much calmer as I descended into the dungeon. Sirene wasn't there, either, and the guard couldn't recall the last time he'd seen her.

By this time, Anissa was starting to worry. "Where could she be? I hope the baby is all right."

All it did was give voice to the concern at the forefront of my thoughts all along. Fane's request that I keep her and the baby safe rang in my ears as we picked up the speed with which we searched.

"Jonah! Here!"

In one of the small alcoves which peppered the ground level of the building, a small splash of blood had already half-dried on the stone floor.

"No..." I looked around, panicking all over again. This couldn't be happening.

"Where would she go?" Anissa asked as we jogged side-by-side.

"I have no idea. I don't know how long it takes a half-vampire, half-witch baby to come to term." I glanced at her from the corner of my eye.

"How would I know?"

"I thought you might have an idea, is all."

"Remember, I didn't know I was half-fae until not long ago. I've never known a woman pregnant with a hybrid—at least, not that I was aware of at the time."

"Of course. I'm just grasping at straws."

A pitiful excuse, but true nonetheless. I was at sea, totally unaware of what the true emergency was. If the baby was early, that would only put more strain on Sirene—and she didn't need any extra complications, as delivery could kill her under the best circumstances.

"Poor Sirene," she whispered, rubbing her hands together in anxiety. "She's all alone somewhere. Do you think she'd go to the high-rise on her own?"

"Maybe. Though she'd be running the risk of crossing paths with somebody less friendly than me." But if she was in labor, she'd want to be someplace more comfortable than headquarters—and more welcoming.

"Should we course back there?"

We stepped out of the building, and the sight of miles of abandoned, overgrown space in all directions did little to soothe my nerves.

Or Anissa's, judging from the way she plucked at her fingernails. "It will take a little time to get there, but it's better than wasting any further time here."

"It makes sense," I admitted, although it didn't feel quite right to me. Some instinct urged me to stay put, to keep searching. I was never the type to pay heed to superstition or anything like it, but there was no denying some force larger than myself held me in place. The presence of her baby, my half-sibling?

Who knew what an unborn witch or warlock was capable of?

A soft groan floated to my ears on the breeze. Anissa's, too, as our eyes locked a moment later.

She was here, somewhere. Nearby.

2

ANISSA

"Sirene?" I cupped my hands around my mouth and turned in the direction it seemed the groan had come from. There was almost no way of telling for certain, though, since the cry was so soft.

Jonah scoured the ground for more blood, half-crouching as he went.

"Here." He pointed, and sure enough, there were a few drops of blood in the dirt.

We followed the trail, him scanning for blood and me looking for her, when I caught sight of the hem of a robe protruding from a clump of tall weeds.

"There!" I was running before I even spoke, breathless with worry.

Sirene was on the ground, curled into a ball, arms crossed over her belly. Sweat stuck her hair to the sides of her face, forehead, and neck.

The sight was chilling. I had never seen her anything less than calm, in control. The pain of labor had torn all of that apart, leaving her vulnerable and whimpering like a wounded animal as she rocked back and forth on the ground.

Her already fair skin was as white as a sheet. "The... baby..." she whispered between groans.

"I know, I know. We're here now. You're not alone." Jonah joined me, kneeling at her side, appearing about as confused and hopeless as I felt.

"I was... trying to portal to the high rise," she gasped.

"That was good thinking. I'm glad we found you before you got there, though," Jonah murmured.

He had gone from being nearly frantic with stress to calm and reassuring.

I wanted to tell him that was the sign of a true leader, that he need never question himself, but it wasn't the time. I would have to remember for later.

Our eyes met.

"What are we supposed to do?" I mouthed.

He shrugged, then gazed down at her again before helping her to a semi-seated position. She leaned against him, arms still wrapped protectively around her swollen belly as she grimaced in pain. My heart ached for her.

"Just... let me catch my breath..." she groaned, eyes squeezed tight. "And we can go."

"I wish there was something we could do for the pain," I offered, feeling completely useless.

"So do I," she gasped, then let out a short laugh.

Even then, in obvious agony, she tried to bring levity for our sake. I could see why Fane cared for her as he did. She wasn't only beautiful, powerful, and kind. She was brave. A man like him would feel the pull of a brave woman like her.

It was clear she wouldn't be able to walk; she could barely sit up without gasping in pain.

"Do you think it would be all right if I carry you?" Jonah asked.

"Yes. I don't want to bring my child into the world out

here." She draped an arm around his neck, and he lifted her gently, slowly, wincing whenever she did.

Even with the situation being as dire as it was, I couldn't help noticing how sweet he was to her. Was it because he liked her for herself, or his father's wishes?

The thought of Fane sent a shiver down my spine. He should've been here. He would want to be. But he had other things to do and didn't want her to know about the change Elazar brought about in him.

Would Fane ever see Sirene again? Would she make it through this?

Sirene raised one hand, closing her eyes as she did. Her brows knit together as she concentrated.

I had never seen her or anyone with the ability to create portals work so hard to do so, but this was a different story.

The portal started as a small, swirling ball of light no bigger than the size of my fist, but slowly grew until it was large enough for us to go through.

"Hurry," she groaned through gritted teeth. "Not sure… how long I can hold it…"

Jonah wasted no time carrying her through, with me right on his heels. In the blink of an eye, we were standing on the balcony outside the penthouse.

The wind took my breath away, and I fought to adjust to the sudden change of location. It was late in the evening, the lights of the city shone as brightly as ever. No one down on the ground, hundreds of feet below us, had any idea what was happening over their heads.

The penthouse was dark, for the most part. I held up a hand to keep Jonah and Sirene at bay while I tiptoed over to the double doors. A quick glance inside told me there was a light burning in one of the bedrooms with the door slightly open to allow a sliver of a beam into the hall.

Otherwise, the living area was dark and empty.

Process of elimination told me it had to be Philippa. Scott was with Fane. And Gage... Nobody knew where Gage was, which seemed to be par for the course. It had been for as long as I'd been acquainted with the family, at any rate.

I waited a few breathless moments to be certain Jonah's sister wouldn't come strolling down the hall before waving Jonah on.

"Philippa," I mouthed, pointing.

His deep frown told me his thoughts ran in the same general direction as mine. Could she be trusted? Given my druthers, I would immediately vote *No*, but much of that was personal. I wouldn't put anything past her.

"Downstairs," he decided. "There's an empty apartment I was going to recommend Sirene stay in, anyway. Let's be as quiet as we can while walking through."

He looked down at Sirene, who was all but writhing in pain.

"Wait..." She grimaced, gritting her teeth as another fresh wave of pain swept over her.

Even in the chill air with the wind whipping around us, there was sweat on her brow. Once the contraction had passed, she nodded. We didn't have much time.

I opened the door for Jonah to slip through. His feet barely seemed to touch the floor as he darted across the room. I was used to sneaking in and out of rooms, apartments, wherever, but Jonah's dexterity surprised me.

We were at the front door in seconds, having escaped notice. I was careful to open it without a creak, lifting it slightly to relieve any weight on the hinges, and we were in the hall.

"Where to?" I whispered.

"Downstairs. Below this one."

"Won't anybody up here be able to hear?" I pressed the button for the elevator.

"Soundproofing. It's pretty thorough." Yet, he didn't seem convinced. If Sirene screamed...

Well, what was the worst that could happen? I told myself it would be all right; Philippa was a woman and would be sympathetic to another woman's pain. I only hoped I wasn't kidding myself as we bundled Sirene into the apartment.

It was furnished, at least, with a king-sized bed in the master suite. Jonah was as careful as could be in lowering her to the mattress while I made sure there were enough pillows behind her.

Then the truth hit me: I had no idea what to do now we had made her as comfortable as we could.

Neither did Jonah, obviously. We exchanged a worried look from opposite sides of the bed.

Sirene opened her eyes and sized up the situation in a glance. "I've assisted in many births," she told us with a grimace. "I can be of help, to a point."

"What do we need?"

She gave us a list of things. Towels, cool water, and a cloth for her head, ice or something for her to sip on.

"Is there anything you know of which we can give you for pain?" I whispered, leaning close to her ear.

I'd already placed towels beneath her, with Jonah discreetly turning his head away.

She sighed. "I wish... there were. But any potion or tonic which would alleviate the discomfort would be—" Her cry was louder than ever before, and her hand darted out to grip mine painfully.

I wouldn't have pulled away for the world; if she could deal with pain as well as she had, I could grit my teeth and struggle through.

When the hurt passed, she fell back against the pillows with her eyes closed. I had the feeling I knew what she had tried to say. She would need a witch to create something for her, or a warlock. Some sort of healer. I couldn't exactly run to a drug store to purchase something for her.

Her hair was already soaked with perspiration, and more of it stuck to her face and forehead. I dipped a cloth in the cool water basin Jonah had brought in, wiping her down as best I could. She managed a weak smile before grimacing again.

The pains were coming faster. They seemed stronger. What were we going to do when the baby started coming?

Jonah paced at the other end of the room, watching us all the while. The life of his baby brother or sister was hanging in the balance, not to mention Sirene's. I wanted to believe he was anxious because he cared more deeply than he had the words to express. I needed to believe that.

When he looked at me, eyes burning into mine, I knew it was true. He cared more than he knew he had up to this moment. He'd been kind and considerate of Sirene because his father had asked him to do so, but watching her as she groaned and whimpered, squeezing my hand until the bones ground together and I bit my tongue to keep from crying out, changed the stakes.

"We need someone else to be here," he decided. "Someone to help with the pain and make sure everything that can be done is being done."

Sirene took a deep breath, eyes squeezed shut. "No one would. No one."

"Oh, that can't be true. If we can convince—"

"There isn't time!" she gasped, then nearly doubled over with a contraction that wrenched a deep, almost animal growl from inside her.

VINDICATION

The sound struck fear into my heart, cold and sharp. My vision blurred before I realized I was crying.

She was going to die right there in this bed, with no one of her kind willing to help her because the baby she carried was half-vampire. Just because of that. It didn't matter what good she'd done, how many she had helped with her powers.

All of my memories came back, mixed with my fear for her. Being ignored, left to my own devices, my sister forced to break the law in order to support us. Thrown into a dungeon and left to starve because none of the Carvers would help us with the basic day-to-day matter of survival.

Sirene had to live. Her child had to have a mother to protect it. I had already lost my mother twice I thought, as I sat on the edge of this bed, holding the witch's hand and wiping the sweat from her brow.

Somebody had to think about the baby.

I looked down at her then at Jonah. "I'll do everything I can to help you. I swear."

GAGE

Plink, plink. Plink, plink.

The ever-present sound of dripping water. Dripping from where? It would be better to ask where water wasn't dripping from, as the sound seemed to be coming from all around me. All the time. Driving me crazy.

I closed my eyes, shutting them tight, willing myself not to hear that which was in every corner of my brain. Like the sound of a heartbeat, but couldn't forget the sound, nor push it to the rear of my consciousness. Because there was nothing else to think about, nothing to distract me.

Except hunger.

Despair.

Betrayal.

Rage.

It seemed no matter how I sliced my situation, there was no aspect worth focusing on for very long. Nothing to comfort me. Not even the thought that Micah would surely take care of Cari—which he would, I had no doubt.

That didn't help one bit. I knew what his idea of caring

for her was, and it only made me want to kill him. He thought he could touch her, kiss her...?

I opened my eyes, now looking around for something to take my mind off the mental image of the two of them together. There had to be something to push those thoughts out of my head. Something, anything.

The rats in the corner, perhaps. Not necessarily something worth focusing on. In fact, something I'd rather pretend didn't exist except in dire situations such as the one I was in, when if I didn't get my thoughts under control, I'd love my sanity.

There were three of them, slipping in and out of a small crevice in the stone wall. I could only guess the wall divided my cell from the one beside it. I could further guess that all of the walls were in the same state of disrepair, and if I worked long enough and patiently enough, I might even be able to tear a hole into one.

To what purpose? All of that work, and all it would lead me to was another cell. And another. I wouldn't be able to get out.

Not that I hadn't tried. The outer walls which comprised the prison—which was what I'd come to think of it as, because what else was I supposed to think?—were carved from solid rock, well underground. The only small window sat at the top of the cell, barred, and revealing nothing. No sound coming from outside, no footfalls or murmured voices or engines.

Nothing.

Who wouldn't watch the rats, then?

They seemed afraid of me, as if they sensed what I was in their animal way. It didn't keep them out of my cell, but it did keep them away from me. As I never slept, I didn't have to worry about them approaching while I was deep in a happy dream.

That would've been the ultimate slap in the face, I decided. Dreaming of a happy time, a happy place, only to wake up and find a rat gnawing on the hem of my pants. Or my flesh.

They skittered away, squeaking and chattering at each other. There were so many other such noises. I generally tried to tune them out.

But that wasn't worse than the silence from outside. This was what truly disturbed me. It meant there was no hope of being heard. No hope of discovery.

No hope of Cari ever finding me, like she saved me the first time when she found me in the canyon, dumped there to die when the sun rose.

In the first few days, I had yelled and roared and cursed Micah and fate itself for putting me in my situation. I had railed against everything against me and sworn vengeance. Blood would flow.

That had been nothing more than a waste of energy. I ended up hoarse and thirsty, with nothing to do about it. And my thirst had only gotten worse as the hours had ticked by.

I sat on the floor with my back against the wall of my cell, looking out at the dimly lit corridor.

"Cari, where are you?" I whispered, unable to get her out of my mind. The scent of her, the feel of her skin. The sound of her voice, the sparkle in her eyes. We had come such a long way from that first night, the night I'd picked up on her scent and followed her.

What had been the point? All it did was get her brutalized, and all but killed. I'd turned her because of it. And we'd become hunted. I'd ended up left for dead.

What was the purpose, if only pain and utter misery had resulted?

She would never find me here. I didn't even know if she would want to, after spending enough time with Micah. He would capitalize on her newness, her freshness, the fact that her thirst was still so sharp and demanding. He would give her what she wanted, instead of making the mistake I made by trying to dampen her spirits.

She would fall deeper into his world—the sleekness of it, the seductiveness of the city.

Once enough time had passed, she'd forget me entirely. And he would allow that—nay, he'd encourage it. Anything he could do to put a wedge between us, even without my being there, he would do.

Plink, plink. Plink, plink.

The dripping water again. The only sounds I'd ever hear for the rest of my long, tortured life.

Along with the sound of my moans and cries and pleas for blood. Because I knew, the lust for blood, the need to feed, to have that life-sustaining essence would overcome soon.

Pleas that no one would hear.

4

CARI

I couldn't stop crying.

For three days, I was either tearing up, actively sobbing, or struggling to stop crying. At least, that was how it seemed.

Gage.

Gage!

What was happening to him? What sort of torture was he going through? What were they doing to him in order to try to get to me?

They would stop at nothing. He hadn't told me too much about the league—he'd avoided specifics pretty strictly—but I knew they were ruthless. I knew they drew a hard line when it came to creating new vampires. They wanted me, and they would use him to get to me.

He'd never let that happen. He would die before he'd give me away.

I let out a guttural moan, sinking into a chair beside Micah's bed.

He'd insisted I stay in his room in the days following

Gage's kidnapping. We didn't share it, he never even suggested it. But he sat up watching me as I tried to rest.

Until now, I had only soaked his pillows with my tears.

I looked at those pillows, at the bed, as I sat alone.

He was someplace, I couldn't remember where. I had hardly paid attention, which was unforgivably rude after he'd been so kind and considerate. So protective.

I would never let anything like that happen to you. They will never find you. I'll protect you. We all will.

I reminded myself of his words, which he had repeated like a prayer in my ear, over and over, since Gage disappeared into that car. I wished I had seen it but was glad I hadn't at the same time. I didn't want my last memories of him to be of his terror or pain as they shoved him into some random car and drove away.

Taking him away from me forever.

I bent forward, covering my face with my hands and rocking back and forth. What was I going to do? How was I supposed to go on without him?

"Cari."

A familiar voice.

Micah knelt in front of me, rubbing my back as I continued to rock.

"Cari, you know how it tears at my heart when I see you like this."

"How do you think I feel when I imagine what Gage is going through?" I wept, not bothering to look at him. He had seen me in various states of hysteria over three days and didn't need to see my tear-stained, swollen face again.

"You're torturing yourself," he murmured, as steady and patient as always.

I wondered how he managed that. He always seemed so

level, where I was frantic and emotional. But he hadn't just lost his love, had he?

My love. My mate, for God's sake. The one I was meant to be with. We were supposed to be together!

Another broken cry wrenched itself from my chest, and when Micah pulled me into his arms, I didn't push away. I was too weak, too tired to fight. And I did need the comfort he promised.

"Shh." He stroked my hair, his arms firm around me. It was nice, feeling taken care of. And immediately, guilt pulled me to pieces all over again. No one was taking care of Gage. He was suffering, maybe dying.

Because of me.

"It's all my fault! All of it!" My chest hurt, actually ached, like someone was squeezing my heart. I wished they would tighten their grip and kill me and get it over with.

"How can you say such a thing?"

"I've been thinking and thinking about it, and there's no other answer."

"So stop thinking about it." He pulled back far enough to take my face in his hands. "Carissa. You're driving yourself mad. You obsess and break your own heart. You break your mind. I can't allow this."

"I don't want to live without him, Micah. He's the only reason I'm still here, still breathing. He made the ultimate sacrifice for me."

"And what would that sacrifice be for if you were to now squander what he gave up his freedom for?" He tucked my hair behind my ears with gentle fingers, a warm smile playing on his lips. He was so good at pretending to be brave for my sake.

I knew it had to be hard on him, knowing his old friend was suffering unimaginably.

"I guess that's true. He would hate that."

"He would. And do you know what else he would hate?"

"What?"

"If he knew how broken up you've been over him. He wouldn't want to see you torturing yourself. He wouldn't want to see those beautiful eyes so bloodshot and swollen with tears. The pink tinged tracks of your tears on your face. He would want to see you going on, taking care of yourself. Making sure he didn't sacrifice in vain."

I sighed, knowing he was right but not feeling very good about it. "It's impossible. I can't just forget about him, and I can't leave him in the hands of whoever has taken him."

"We know who took him."

"I mean, specifically, who took him. Where they put him. I can't leave him there. He needs me."

His eyes widened and hardened. He rose. "I don't think you know what you're saying."

"I know exactly what I'm saying." I stood, too, facing him. For once, I wasn't crying. "I want to find him. I want to rescue him."

"That's insanity. That's what you're speaking of right now. Insanity."

"I'm sorry you feel that way, but it doesn't change my mind."

"Cari, Cari." He took my arms in his large hands then shook his head. "You don't know who you're up against. Drop this idea. Drop it and forget you ever had it. It's far too dangerous for both of you."

"I can't sit here in comfort, with you and the others, knowing what he's going through!"

"But think, *cheri*. Really think. They want you just as much as they want him—perhaps more, because, to them, you are a monster. Something which should never have been."

I winced, turning my face away.

"I'm sorry to be so harsh with you, but it's true. Have you considered they might be lying in wait for you, right now, as we speak?"

"Of course." I sat down again when my knees went weak. It made perfect sense—sick, perfect sense. They could've been using him as a way to draw me in, to lure me. He was the bait in their trap.

"I know that's difficult to hear." He sat on the edge of the bed, one hand on my shoulder. "Please, you must promise me something."

"What? You want me to promise not to lose my head again? To stop dissolving into tears at the drop of a hat? You're tired of seeing me so emotional, so on edge all the time?"

He winced, shaking his head. "You're very tough on yourself, you know. I wasn't going to say any of those things."

I blushed, feeling roughly as big as an ant. Grief and panic were turning me into a shrew. My human side still overrode my vampire side, sometimes. "Oh. What, then?"

"I wanted you to promise not to entertain any thoughts of rescuing Gage."

"I see." I shook off the hand still resting on my shoulder. "I don't like being told what I'm allowed to think. Especially when I'm so upset I hardly know which end is up. If you'll excuse me, I want to go back to my own room for a little while. I need to be alone."

"Cari. Wait..."

"No, please." I held up a hand, holding it between us when he tried again to put his arms around me. As comforting as his touch was, I didn't want him getting the wrong idea about my boundaries.

And I needed to firm up those boundaries. It was too easy

to let him comfort me. A slippery slope I couldn't allow myself to slide down.

"I hate to think of you being alone right now," he murmured, caressing me with his voice the way he always did.

Normally, I appreciated it. Right now, he made me furious.

"I know what I need. I've known myself much longer than you have, Micah." I stalked out of the room and down the dark, narrow tunnel leading to my room. The room I had shared with Gage.

It didn't even have a door. I was never truly alone, never able to block out the rest of the clan. I could close the beaded curtain which stood for a door and pretend it meant something, but all it did was block most of the light and none of the sound.

I could still hear the low murmur of chatter farther down in the tunnel, coming from a common room where several of the others enjoyed gathering. Naomi's voice rang out clearly, rich and strong. She was a natural leader. When she spoke, people listened.

The pillow still smelled like Gage. I buried my face in it, holding it close to me, clinging desperately to anything that represented him. I had nothing without him. It was so clear. What was I thinking, fighting it the way I had? Pushing him away? I would've given anything to take it all back. Anything.

Even my life, which meant nothing without him in it.

"Cari?"

I lifted my face from the pillow with a sigh. "Yes?"

"I didn't want to leave things the way they were," Micah murmured from the other side of the curtain. "Might I come in?"

"Of course." It was strange, thinking of the tunnels as his.

They weren't his. But it still felt as though I was living in his home, and it would be rude to ask him to leave me alone.

He kept his distance, hovering by the arch carved into the rock. "I'm sorry for upsetting you back there. I know what it means to want to rescue the person you care most about in the world. I still remember it all too well."

I softened. "What an idiot I am. Oh, Micah, I'm sorry. I keep forgetting you've been through something like this before."

He nodded slowly, his arms folded across his chest. "I wanted to go after her, too. I wanted to make them all pay for thinking they could so much as touch her. It all but tore my heart from my chest, knowing the pain she was in, knowing how terrified she must have been. Knowing there was nothing I could do about any of it. That feeling of complete helplessness."

"Yes," I whispered.

"And all because of me."

"That's exactly how I feel."

"But you didn't do anything," he reminded me. "Cari, you didn't ask for any of this. Gage made his choice, and I'm sure he would make it again if given the chance."

I sat up, swinging my legs over the side of the bed. "I don't know about that."

When he sat beside me, I didn't move away. He reached for me, touching a strand of hair which had come loose from the bun at the nape of my neck. "I can't see how he could've chosen otherwise. In his place, I would've done the same thing. How could I not?"

I ducked my head, strangely uncomfortable but comforted at the same time. It felt good to be touched, to be consoled.

It also felt like I was betraying Gage.

Micah, oblivious to what was going on in my head, was still comforting me. "I don't know what I would do without you now. That might not be right, and I'm sorry if it seems disrespectful, but I can't help it. You're special to me. I feel as though… Well, I feel as though you were meant to be here. If Gage was going to be captured, this is the best place for you to possibly be. You're safe. You're cared for. You're valued. You're one of us."

One of them.

Was I? I wanted to be—or thought I did, at first. When we'd hunted together and I felt so alive. I belonged then.

How did I ever think it mattered without Gage?

Micah draped an arm around my shoulders, drawing me into a hug.

I allowed my head to rest against his shoulder—it was nice, and he did care. Gage wouldn't mind. He would want me to find comfort where I could. He'd be glad to know I wasn't crying, for at least a little while.

Wouldn't he?

5

MICAH

What the hell was it going to take for her to forget about him?

I held her as close as I dared, highly aware of how sensitive she was. She was still human enough to feel unfaithful whenever we were too close. I sensed it in the way her body changed, the way lines appeared between her brows when she struggled to contain a frown.

I was so certain she'd fall into my arms. What was going wrong? There was nothing like planning something and envisioning it going a certain way, then watching everything fall apart. None of the joy I'd expected to experience had come to fruition.

Though knowing Gage suffered, alone and in the dark, that helped somewhat.

"Promise me," I whispered in her ear as she rested against me.

She smelled of sweetness, freshness. Vitality. Everything I had missed for so long. The scent brought back memories long since hidden deep in my heart.

"Promise what?" she whispered, her voice still thick with tears.

Wasn't she tired of crying yet?

"Promise you won't try to find him." I cupped her chin in my palm, lifting it so our eyes met.

She was luminous, radiating light and beauty and purity. Even after crying her vampire tears. Especially after that. Her lips were swollen, her expression vulnerable. I nearly ached with the need to kiss her.

"It's really that important to you, isn't it?"

"What a silly question." I smiled, my barely retracted fangs tight against the inside of my lips. "Yes. It is that important to me, *cheri*. You are that important. I can't lose you now. You're my responsibility—and, if you don't mind my admitting it, my salvation."

"Salvation?" she echoed, frowning.

I sighed as though it were a secret I was hesitant to share with her. I even averted my eyes, looking down at the floor. "There are... many things which I've struggled against lately. A feeling of uselessness. Sameness. Never being able to leave this closed-in place which reeks of centuries of death. I know you can smell it, too. Don't pretend you don't."

She laughed softly. "I won't, then."

"I miss being part of the world," I continued. "I realize our kind can't be in the world the way humans are. I know I'll never feel the sun on my skin again. I resigned myself to that long ago. It was more the loneliness which ate at me."

"Lonely? Here, among all the others?"

"It isn't the same as feeling... connected."

"I know what you mean." We sat in silence for several seconds, as I waited for her to pick up the message of what I was trying to explain. She didn't—or, even worse—she didn't feel compelled to speak up.

What was it going to take?

One of the worst things I could do was push too hard. She had already pulled away once.

"I'll leave you alone now. I know you want some time on your own. But please, whatever you need. You know where to find me."

"Thank you." She sat with her shoulders slumped, hands clasped in her lap as I walked out into the tunnel.

Part of me did feel sorry for her as I headed back to my room. She looked so lost.

Naomi was waiting for me, stretched out on her side across the bed. "Fancy meeting you here," she murmured with a wide smile. "It's been a while."

"And I don't recall telling you it was safe to come to my room right now." I ducked my head back out into the tunnel, making certain Cari wasn't heading my way.

"Relax. She's in there, crying over Gage. Which is exactly where I warned you she would be if you pulled any of your tricks."

I glared at her. "You'd better watch the words coming from your mouth. You ought to know better by now than to test me."

"Come, come. Since when are we such bad friends?" She pushed herself up on one elbow.

In the light from the candles Cari had lit at some point, her dark skin seemed to glow with an entrancing energy. I had always been a sucker for Naomi's beauty, not to mention her charm and composure. And her wicked sense of humor.

I was in no joking mood, as I sat on the bed and took her chin in my hand. Just as I had with Cari only minutes earlier, only without the tenderness I had shown Cari.

"What are you driving at, *cheri*? Are you trying to say I

arranged this somehow? That what happened to Gage is my fault?"

Her wide, clear, frank eyes stared into mine. She didn't flinch, didn't cringe. She showed no hint of reaction to my growing ire.

"Well? What is it?"

She was maddening. I never could see into her head the way I could see into others' heads. It wasn't clairvoyance, exactly, but rather an ability to read expressions and the motivation behind a person's tone of voice. It was a gift I'd used even in my human days.

It was useless against her.

"Nothing at all, Micah," she whispered, speaking slowly, deliberately. "I must have been mistaken."

"You're right, you must've been." I dropped her chin and all but shoved her away. "Sometimes, I think you forget your position in my life."

She sat up, crossing her long legs with a graceful movement. "And what position would that be, exactly? It always seems to change, depending on your mood."

"I told you to watch yourself."

"And I've told you many, many times I don't like being told what to do." She smiled, but there was an edge to it. "Even by you, *mon cher*."

It was time to stop playing games. "Was there any other reason for you to visit?"

Her eyes narrowed. "What do you think? Why do I need any special reason? I never needed one before, did I?"

"No..."

Her hand slid up my arm, reaching my shoulder. "I've been all on my own for weeks now, ever since they arrived."

"I thought you liked Cari."

"Oh. I do. Very much. But I mean, she's no substitute for you." She ran her fingers around the curve of my neck.

I flinched away.

"I didn't mean it like that," I snapped.

Her hand returned to rest on my shoulder. "I know how you meant it. I thought you enjoyed my sense of humor." She pouted a little. "I don't know how to take you lately. You're not yourself."

"You know the stress I've been under."

"Stress of your own creation." There was an edge to her voice once again, and a sharpness in her eyes as her fingers dug into my neck, her hand curled around the back of it.

One second, she was caressing me, the next she was ready to crush my bones.

"I fear you don't know your own strength."

"I know my strength." Her eyes were hard again as she leaned closer. I could smell light perspiration on her skin, and the lingering scent of her latest kill. She had been hunting, and recently. That explained her sudden aggressiveness. Or so I told myself.

"What is it you're really trying to say?" I whispered, searching her eyes for some clue. "Since when do you come to my room with the intent of snapping my neck? It isn't normally my neck you're concerned with."

"Stop playing. You don't want me. Stop pretending you do, all to keep me subjugated to you."

Her words stunned me. Not because they weren't true—yes, she helped fulfill my baser needs, but the hours we spent together had gone from an exciting dalliance to a way of keeping her quiet.

It was the fact she knew it which left me chilled to my core.

"Why do you say these words which could only hurt me?"

I whispered, hoping to at least contain her bitterness long enough to solve the problem of what to do with her.

Just like that, the pressure on my neck ceased, and her touch went back to being a caress. Nothing more. "You've hurt me for a long time, Micah," she murmured, her eyes turning pink with unshed tears. They sparkled in the candlelight.

"It was never my intention."

"I'm certain it wasn't." Her hand slid to my chest, which she patted. "You only consider that which is best for you. It isn't that you actively seek to harm those you use in order to achieve your aims. You simply don't consider them at all."

There was simple truth in her words, spoken in the soft, defeated cadence of a woman who had arrived at a sad truth long since and had merely done her best to live with it in the years following.

I chuckled, putting on an air of confusion. "You make me sound like some mastermind. A puppeteer. As if you all dance on the strings which I control."

She shrugged. "Aren't you? Don't we?" She scanned the room without moving her head, those intelligent eyes sweeping over the sparse furnishings. "I think I'd better take to spending every night in my room. Always. Even after you're finished with your new toy."

"Don't call her that," I warned as she stood.

"I like the girl." She sighed, turning toward me. "I truly do. I'm certain if we were both human, living in the same time and place, we would've been friends. I would like to be her friend now, if possible. But we both know that can't be so. Don't we? Because she isn't long for us."

"What makes you say that?" I asked, suddenly intrigued and perhaps a bit apprehensive. What did she know that I didn't? Had Cari been talking with her or any of the others?

"Isn't it obvious? For someone who's made paying attention to the habits and tendencies of others his entire life, you're rather blind when it comes to the simple things."

I frowned.

When it was clear I didn't follow, she sighed heavily once again and folded her lean arms. "Listen. She's not going to be with us long. I feel it in my bones. She'll either make a rash mistake out of grief or rage and get herself caught, or she'll run away in search of her precious Gage. Either way, you will be the one responsible for what becomes of her."

"Me?" I scoffed. "I, who've opened our home to her? I, who took a chance by taking them in? It might have meant ruin for all of us, but I couldn't allow them to flounder without a friend. And you tell me it's my fault should something happen to her?"

"Enough." She sounded tired.

More so than I had ever heard her in the decades since we'd first met.

"Just... enough, Micah. I only ask for your sake, and for hers, you give a great deal of thought to what you may or may not have done. And what it may or may not mean farther down the line."

She cut me off before I had the chance to protest, adding, "I won't stand in your way. I never have before, have I? You've been free to work your plans, pulling the strings as you see fit. But do not expect me to keep quiet when I see such blatant cruelty being perpetrated in front of me. Understood?"

We stared at each other for a long, heavy minute. The only sound in the room was our breathing as we challenged each other.

I'd never thought of Naomi as an opponent before—and, frankly, wasn't certain whether I should think of her as one now, either.

The only wise action, I decided, would be to give in to her terms. No sense in dragging out a pointless argument which might only serve to reveal more of what I'd worked so hard to conceal.

"All right," I agreed. "I understand. And I appreciate your honesty."

Her laugh was rich. "No, you don't. Of all the lies you've ever fed me, Micah, that might be the biggest of all." She was still laughing when she left, the sound echoing after her.

I felt as though I'd been hit by a speeding bus. What was that about? What was she trying to say? That she knew what I'd done to Gage?

Could it mean she knew what I'd done to Xavier, too?

No. That was so long ago. Fifty years, at least. She couldn't still be holding on to that old heartache.

Could she?

I'd held on to Georgina for twice as long. I always would, until I drew my final breath.

6

FELICITY

It pained me to witness Gregor's pain.

Why did fate have to be so cruel? I had never been much of a believer, having seen too much over time to put my faith in some all-knowing force guiding our lives in spite of our choices. I didn't like the notion of there not being a path, but the one our feet started down the day we were born.

Even so, it seemed as though there was a plan at work in our lives, and I didn't like it one bit.

Gregor and Tabitha, for instance.

What was the purpose of their being reunited only to be pulled apart again? Wasn't it enough he'd nursed an undying love for her up to that point? That he would never forget her, that their love came back just as fresh and new as ever every time he looked at their daughter?

No, it wasn't. Not for the force which had brought them back together again. He had hoped. He'd become almost a new man, one I'd hardly recognized. A childlike gleam had shone in his eyes. He'd hoped.

He had hoped.

Which made his fresh heartache all the more potent. The half-healed wound was torn open and deeper than ever.

I watched him from my seat on the other side of the hearth.

We'd sat in silence since Anissa and Jonah left, unable to muster the energy for conversation.

What was there to discuss? Certainly, we could talk about the wedding, but it only brought up the question of whether Tabitha would be present for it.

We both knew she wouldn't be.

Though he did a good job of showing enthusiasm while they were with us. In their absence, he seemed to fold in on himself. A shadow of the man I once knew, someone I'd butted heads with more times than I could count. He didn't appear to have any of the old bluster in him as he stared into the fire.

"It will be a beautiful wedding," I ventured, choosing my words carefully. "They're a beautiful couple."

"They are. It will." He leaned back against the cushions behind him and exhaled.

"You're a good father for wanting to give her a lovely day. She deserves it. She's strong and brave. Like someone I know." I flashed him a small, tentative smile, which he returned. A good sign.

"I wonder how brave," he sighed. "I don't feel very brave at the moment. I feel useless, weak. As though there was nothing I could've done to protect..." He couldn't say her name. It would've made everything too real.

"Perhaps there was nothing you could've done at all, no matter what. There were other forces at work in this. I hope we find out one day who or what was behind this. I hate to think of the culprit going unpunished."

"I would never allow it," he vowed, his eyes flashing as a bit of the old Gregor came out.

"I know you wouldn't. But so long as we know nothing about what went on, what's the chance the responsible party will ever pay for what they did?" I tented my fingers beneath my chin, elbows on the arms of my chair.

We fell into yet another long, stormy silence.

Allonic may have been able to help, if he hadn't disappeared. The fact he was missing at the same time as his mother didn't do much to soothe my already frayed nerves. Had something happened to both of them at once? Was the blood we'd found not just Tabitha's blood? What if he had gone there in search of her and whoever or whatever had killed Tabitha had been waiting...?

I ground my teeth together as I imagined this. I knew I shouldn't, it would get me nowhere, but there was no stopping once I'd started. The image of their lifeless bodies, lying side by side... It made me sick, sent my pulse racing, and turned my stomach.

My heart ached.

What was there for us? Gregor and me? Sitting together in his chambers for the rest of our lives, waiting for our loves to come back to us? We'd grow old there, decaying as time spun on, keeping a silent vigil for those who would never return.

There was another possibility, too, one which didn't please me much more than the thought of Allonic dying—the idea he'd never loved me. That I had been nothing more than a pleasant diversion to him. Why else would he stay away for so long?

Gregor's tired voice broke through the stillness. "I don't know what to do anymore. I feel as though we've exhausted every possibility. There's no chance of finding someone to explore ShadesRealm for us—not without risking Garan's ire."

"Garan," I muttered. The short meeting with the ruler of ShadesRealm hadn't instilled much faith. "He didn't seem to care at all, did he?"

Gregor shrugged. "It's not easy, ruling as we do. On the one hand, I understand. He has many concerns which need his time and attention. Let's not forget he lost his father, too. There was a lot on his mind during our visit. The condition of a single person—not even a shade, on top of everything else—was rather low on his list of priorities."

"Right, which means it's up to us to do something about this."

"Felicity." He turned a tired eye to me, shaking his head. "What else is there to do? There are certain lines a leader cannot cross without taking the consequences not only on his shoulders, but upon the shoulders of those he protects. If I were to incur Garan's ire, the result would not only be mine to shoulder. Do you understand what I'm trying to say?"

"Fine," I said, leaning forward. My blood stirred, my mind spun. "If you don't want to do it, I will."

"I don't agree with this."

"I understand. You don't have anything to do with my decision. And should the worst happen, should I be discovered, you can claim to know nothing about my presence in ShadesRealm."

"He'll never believe that."

"He'll have to, once you deny knowledge of my movements."

He winced as though this was unthinkable. "You want me to deny you? I don't know if I could do that, Felicity. It would feel as though I was denying part of my family."

He'd never spoken of me that way, and my heart warmed

at his words. It didn't matter, though, not when there was something larger at stake.

"You'll simply have to try," I decided, standing. "I'm going to go. We shouldn't speak of it again. You can answer with some degree of honesty that you don't know when I went or what my plans were."

He stood, too, coming to me with his hands extended. "I could forbid this, you know."

"You don't truly want to, do you?" I asked, barely holding back a smile.

He wanted me to go, even against his better judgment. He wanted to know what happened to Tabitha as much as I did.

What he didn't know was how determined I was to find Allonic while I was there. It would sound too selfish if I were to announce my full intentions, so I kept them to myself. Dishonest, perhaps, but he would only worry more if he knew.

The fact he hadn't deduced this on his own betrayed the true depth of his grief. He never would've let me get away with a half-truth before. He was too sharp, his mind too probing. He would've raked me over the coals until I'd admitted the truth of my plans.

Now, after losing his love for the second time, he was a shadow of the sharp, infuriating man.

"I'll get my things together and leave shortly," I announced.

His jaw worked as he decided the most diplomatic choice of words. I'd seen that expression many times over the years.

Finally, all he said was, "Please. Be careful."

"I won't let Avellane down."

"I'm not referring only to Avellane," he informed me in his gruff voice, blustering his way through the warmth of his emotions as always. "I'm concerned about you. Be careful for your own sake, more than anything else. I can take care of Avellane."

"Of course you can." We left it at that, with me hurrying from his chambers moments later.

My pulse raced. There were too many thoughts racing through my head all at once for me to focus on one at a time. I was going to ShadesRealm. Was taking a bigger chance than I'd ever taken in my entire life. Never had I ever put myself or anyone else at such risk.

Was I up to the challenge?

I locked myself in my chambers and immediately went to the chest where I kept my tonics and healing tinctures. It had been a long time since I'd needed to use any of them, and there was no guarantee I'd need any of them on my journey. I hoped not. I would rather not run into trouble, and I certainly didn't want to treat my own injuries.

Still, it was best to be prepared.

My skin tingled in anticipation, every muscle tensed and ready. What would I find there? Where should I start? At the tower, I supposed. There had to be some clue there as to who had visited the tower while Tabitha was there.

As unlikely as I knew it to be, I couldn't shake the hope Allonic would be waiting there. He might be in hiding, with information as to who killed Tabitha. It could've been one of the shades, perhaps one of Garan's own men.

Was there a correlation between Garan's father Ressenden's death and Tabitha's? Had Garan only been allowing her to live in ShadesRealm while his father was in power?

If that was the case, it meant if Allonic was alive, he might be in danger as well. Garan might have plans for him. It would've made sense for him to stay hidden.

Hope bloomed in my chest. Dangerous hope. I wondered

if I should allow it—hadn't Gregor held hope, after finding Tabitha again? Hadn't he planned out an entire life for the two of them? I knew he had, even if he hadn't admitted it. He didn't need to admit it.

The voice of reason in my head chided me. *You're kidding yourself. Stop grasping at straws.*

I sat back on my heels, on the floor in front of my chest. Was I? Was I behaving as irrationally as Gregor had? Allowing myself to believe pretty fantasies so long as it meant not having to believe Allonic had never cared about me?

Was it really better to imagine Allonic being in danger than to imagine him never caring for me?

Darkness settled over my thoughts. If he was in hiding, why would he stay in ShadesRealm? Would he flee somewhere safer? The human world, where his sister would likely be?

My heart sank. Yes. That was a greater probability.

Which led me to the two possibilities I'd wrestled with for endless hours in Gregor's chambers.

Either something terrible had happened to Allonic, or he'd never cared for me and had no intention of returning from ShadesRealm.

Regardless of which was true, I wondered if I would ever get over the pain. Would I face the rest of my days the way Gregor would, always wondering what might have been?

I closed the chest then sighed as I rose, sliding my arms into the cloak which held vials and bottles in the pockets sewn inside. I was as ready as I'd ever be.

I hoped.

7

SCOTT

What I wished more than anything was to understand when things had changed.

Where was I when it happened? What was I thinking, what was I doing? How long had it taken? Here I was, worrying about Sara and asking anyone who would listen if they knew where she'd gone. Like a fool. Like her lapdog, running around after her, wanting nothing more than to be with her.

And what was she doing all along? Betraying me. Lying about who she truly was. Letting me go on with the belief she was like me, that she wanted me. That she wanted us.

All the while, training with another man. All the while, making a fool out of me. Letting me want her and long for her and worry about her.

A witch. Nothing but a witch. That's what she was. A damned elemental witch.

I wished I knew when it happened. I had never known such embarrassment—but then again, I had never loved before. There had never been anyone in my life but her. And look where it got me, finally offering myself to someone.

I glared at her from beneath lowered brows as she whispered with that warlock of hers.

Stark.

Just the thought of his name made me curl my lip in a snarl. Who did he think he was, sealing me in ice, making an even bigger fool out of me?

And she didn't try to stop him. She never once told him he shouldn't have done it. She let it happen, the treacherous…

What went wrong?

And how did I ever think the sight of her made me happy? All she did was turn my stomach.

Where was Fane? I couldn't get off the island without him —I'd be damned before I'd ask Sara or Stark for a portal. I didn't know if either of them were capable of creating one. Fane hadn't bothered to tell me where he was going before he disappeared.

Not that I should've been surprised. My dad had been doing that for a long time. Including, letting us think he was dead.

Stark looked at me, our eyes meeting for one rage-inducing second, before he glanced away again. He thought I was intimidated, I guessed. He didn't know I felt sorry for him.

Has she told you she loves you? Has she told you how safe you make her feel? That she doesn't know what she'd do without you in her life? How lost she was before you met?

Does she make you feel like a king, as though there's nothing you can't do with her at your side? Like you're the entire world, just you and nothing matters other than you two? Have you thought about starting a life with her?

Did you nearly start a war over her? Does sheltering her mean danger for you? And are you willing to face that danger because you love her, and she needs you so much? Would you do it without a second's thought because you're the only person who can protect her?

Do you know how good she is at using people?

It was the only way I could explain it—and when I thought of it that way, it was all so clear. Crystal. How could I have ever been so blind? She'd used me. I was her protector. I made it possible for her to live comfortably after the ordeal she'd suffered through.

And then, something better came along.

I wanted to warn him but wasn't foolish enough to think he'd believe me. Too love-struck to listen to reason. I'd been there, under her spell.

What if she had been a witch all along? It wouldn't surprise me a bit. She had sure fooled me.

I turned away from them, finally leaving the castle—not a prison anymore, I guessed, unless Elewyn wanted to keep it that way. Was it only her brother she had wanted to free? She had changed the weather. An improvement. I could breathe more freely outside.

Without having to look at Sara.

What was taking Fane so long? Would he forget I was there, waiting for him?

My bitter chuckle rang out in the otherwise quiet courtyard. Par for the course, at this point. I couldn't think of worse torture than being stuck on Shadowsbane Island with Sara and Stark.

Would Elewyn help me? Only if there was something in it for her, I was willing to bet. Just like her brother.

My skin crawled at the thought of him. Filthy, lying, evil. He was in there somewhere, probably plotting with his sister. Scheming over how to lure yet another unsuspecting victim into a trap.

The sound of Fane's boots slapping against the stones was

the closest thing to music I could imagine. He turned the corner, coming from around the side of the castle.

"What's wrong?" he immediately asked, his eyes shifting in the direction of the open door.

"Nothing."

"You seem as though something's wrong."

I barked out a humorless laugh. "I can't imagine why."

He folded his arms, looking me up and down. "Everyone we care about is alive and well. Sometimes, that's all we can ask for."

"Everyone we care about?" I asked my dad. "You don't know. You have no idea what I went through before you decided to come back into our lives. My history with..." I pointed into the castle.

"You're right. I don't know. But I know you're all right, and Anissa is as well. That could've gone a lot worse than it did, you might be in a cell at this very moment. And it would've been no one's fault but your own."

I snarled at him, stopping just short of baring my fangs, but he didn't blink. His way of telling me he wasn't intimidated. "You can send me home whenever you want. A simple portal will do. I'm sure it's even easier for you to create those now," I couldn't help adding.

He only flashed a tight smile before striding away. "Yes. It is."

I followed him inside, hanging back a bit, watching as he glanced around.

"Where is Elazar?" he asked Sara.

"I'm here." The necromancer stood at the top of the stairs, staring down at all of us with his typical sneer. "Just waiting on you, Fane. I trust you've settled your affairs."

"I have no affairs," Fane replied, shaking of his head. "But I did see to Anissa's safety."

"She's home?" Sara asked.

Her fake sincerity turned my stomach. As if she were capable of caring for anyone, even her sister. The sister she'd led into becoming Marcus's assassin. How many times had she sworn to me it broke her heart, knowing what Anissa had been forced to do for her sake?

"She is," Fane confirmed. "You can rest easy."

"Thank you so much. And good luck with whatever it is you have to do now." Her eyes strayed to where I stood, near the door.

I thought I loved her. Up until the moment I saw her with him, out in the courtyard, I was sure I did. And I was sure she loved me, too. Why would I doubt it? She had told me so many times. Had sworn she'd never leave me.

Hadn't even bothered to tell me when she'd found somebody else.

I couldn't remember everything that happened out there. I'd seen red, I knew that, and the only thing I could think about in those first horrible moments was wanting to kill him for touching her. I had never lost myself to rage before.

Stupid me, thinking she was worth becoming enraged over.

The next thing I knew, I was trapped in ice. It wasn't cold, strangely enough. I'd been perfectly comfortable, other than the way everyone in the prison and standing around me had a prime view of my shame. They all knew I had lost my heart to her, that she had used and discarded me.

I didn't know what was worse: her betrayal or their knowledge of it.

Fane turned to me, blocking my view of Sara and Stark. "Are you ready?"

"I've never been more ready. I want to get home."

"I didn't say you were going home."

I stared at him.

He returned the stare. Challenging me in front of everyone.

I wouldn't make a fool of myself again. I couldn't. "Where am I going?"

"To Duskwood, with Elazar and myself. I need to find a caster, and I can't travel through there with him alongside me. He wouldn't make it a full minute, if seen. No offense," he added, shooting a look Elazar's way.

He shrugged as he walked down the stairs, as though he accepted his fate. He even seemed good-natured about it. "None taken. You only speak the truth."

"I need you to guard him while I'm searching," Fane explained. "I can't risk him running off or being discovered."

"I'm certain I'll feel much safer knowing you're there with me." Elazar smiled, hands clasped behind his back.

I bit my tongue, determined not to let emotion get the better of me again. Any emotion.

"Fine. Let's go, then. I'd rather forget I ever visited this place." I strode outside without so much as a backward glance.

What was she thinking? Did she regret what she'd done? Doubtful. Well, it was better for her to rot on this wretched island.

I wished she would.

Fane took his time following, and I saw why when he came out carrying my mother's body.

A lump formed in my throat.

His face was a mask, completely blank, but his eyes were hard. They seemed to burn.

At least he knew she had loved him.

8

JONAH

It was difficult to say how much time had passed, the blackout curtains hanging over the windows blocked out every last bit of light. Was it morning yet?

It could've been the following evening, for all I knew. It felt that way, as though an entire day had passed. A day of utter agony for the woman on the bed, sweating and bleeding and almost constantly groaning, grunting, or weeping.

No, it couldn't have been that long. No way she would survive for so long. Hours, maybe. It may as well have been forever for her, I was sure.

Guilt wracked me as I searched my thoughts for something I could do to help her.

I wondered, in some deep, dark corner of my mind, if it wouldn't better for her to die sooner rather than later. She surely would, regardless of when. No one could sustain the amount of pain and strain she'd been under and survive. It seemed cruel for her to endure much longer.

That was stupid, of course, and I berated myself for it. I wanted her to live for her sake, for the child's sake. For Fane's sake. I just wished her suffering would end.

"All right. The contractions are less than two minutes apart." Anissa looked at me, eyes wide and circled with dark smudges. Fear had done it to her. She appeared drawn and frail, but she was acting as though she were anything but.

"Does that mean it's time to start pushing?" I asked, completely at a loss.

"I don't know." She glanced at Sirene, who managed to nod.

"I feel... as though I should push..." she gasped.

Her voice was weak. Too weak. I tried not to stare at the small-but-growing stack of bloody towels which Anissa had discarded in favor of fresh ones. Even to my untrained eye, it seemed as though we were going through a lot of them.

"All right." Anissa peered up at me from her position at Sirene's thighs. She had a towel draped over the witch's knees and a light positioned at her elbow so she could see.

Even in the middle of what was likely the deepest fear I had ever felt—the idea of Sirene dying in front of us, with nothing to do about it—I couldn't help but admire the way Anissa took charge.

Just when I thought there was nothing new to learn about her, that I had seen every side of her, she managed to surprise me.

The assassin midwife.

"How should we do this?" she asked Sirene, who seemed to be fading by the minute.

The smell of her blood filled my nostrils, overtaking my senses in a way I was hardly proud of. It couldn't be helped, but I could control it. I stepped closer to the bed, hoping to help in some way now that it seemed as though things were coming to a head.

"I need to sit up..." Her sweaty head rolled from side to

side as she tried to speak. "Think of... a crouch... but lying down..."

"Of course." Anissa pointed to me then to Sirene. "Sit behind her. Prop her up until she's upright." Meanwhile, she lifted Sirene's feet and placed them against her own shoulders. "Brace yourself against me, all right? Just press as hard as you have to."

"Don't want to hurt you," she whispered with a ghost of a smile.

"You'd be surprised how strong I am." Anissa smiled back.

I slid an arm around Sirene's shoulders, as she didn't make a move to sit up on her own. I was afraid she no longer had the strength to do even that much. Her robes were soaked with sweat, as were the sheets beneath her. I sat gingerly, allowing her to lean against me. She felt so light, so easily broken.

I felt I should say something, at any rate, and that it should be reassuring.

"You can do this," I murmured, at a loss for anything else to say.

"I feel..." Her head fell back on my shoulder, her half-closed eyes focused on me. "I feel like I'm dying."

"I'm sure all women feel that way when they're at this stage," Anissa attempted to joke, though the edge in her voice spoke of the dire situation. She removed yet another bloody towel and replaced it with a fresh one.

How much blood could a person lose without...?

Sirene tensed, her breathing coming fast and sharp.

"All right. Here we go..." Anissa shouted, pushing back against the feet on her shoulders.

It felt natural to push Sirene forward, to help her bear down. In the back of my mind, I couldn't help but take note of how surreal the situation was. My baby sibling was on its way into the world as I fumbled my way through, trying to help.

Sirene gasped once she finished pushing, falling against me again.

"Let her rest for a minute," Anissa muttered.

"What's happening?"

"I can barely see the head," she fretted, glancing at Sirene. A frown created deep furrows in her brow. "It's not coming fast enough. Is there any way we can help you?"

Sirene didn't answer. I was afraid she had lost consciousness—or worse.

"Sirene." My voice was loud, sharp, my mouth close to her ear. "We need you to stay with us." I placed a hand on her neck and felt her pulse—weak, but there.

She stirred. "I can't... I can't do it..."

"You will," I ordered. "Your baby needs you to do this. You can't give up now. I won't let you."

"Please... I have to sleep..."

It was unthinkable, seeing her this way. She had always been the one with the answers, the unflappable one. I found myself regretting every bad thought I'd had about her. "Sirene, you have to tell us how to help you. There's got to be something we can do."

It took a moment for her to rouse, and even then, it was only because another contraction was on its way.

I had noticed already how her midsection would seem to tighten whenever one came on, as though her body was trying to push the baby out. I supposed it was.

"Push on me," she managed to groan before she could no longer speak thanks to the animal cry which tore through the room.

I never would've thought a tiny thing like her could make such a sound.

I exchanged a glance with Anissa, who shrugged. There was nothing else to do. I pushed her forward, wrapping my arms around her to press against the top of her swollen belly. It would've been funny if the situation hadn't been so dire—me, trying to push a baby out of a woman.

But it was working. "I see the head! It's coming!" Anissa looked up at Sirene. "Hang on. Just a little while longer."

Sirene gasped for air between contractions, grunting as another came on top of the last.

I pushed harder than ever, afraid for a moment I would hurt her but guessing I couldn't do worse than had already been done to her.

Our priority was to get the baby out, and fast. Before we lost both of them. It didn't have to be spoken aloud for all of us to know it.

"Keep going, keep going... Almost there..." Anissa's voice went up an octave in excitement. "The head's almost out! You're doing it, Sirene! You're doing it!"

"Come on!" I barked. "You got this!"

I gazed down at her, at the sweaty head lolling on my shoulder as she tried valiantly to do it, and something told me I might never get another chance. "I'm sorry for everything. I should've been better. I should've done better. It shouldn't have taken something like this for me to know how stupid I was. You make my father happy—as happy as he can be. I'm glad he's had you in his life. We're all lucky to have you."

"Take care of the baby... please..."

"No! No, you're going to! You will!" I nearly yelled with the effort of pushing for her—and the effort of holding myself together as she faded in my arms.

She was dying. There would be no saving her after this. Her ribs were cracking under my hands, but I couldn't stop pushing because the baby would suffocate if we didn't get it out and we'd lose them both, and oh, how would I ever face Fane after that? Or Anissa?

Or myself?

Sirene screamed once more, louder and stronger than I thought she had the strength to do.

Anissa let out a yelp. "It's here! It's here! Stop pushing!"

I fell back, Sirene coming with me. She was limp but breathing.

"You did it." I put an arm across her chest to hold her against me. Or just to hold her. The closest thing to a hug I could manage. If anyone deserved it, she did.

"Thank you. Thank you." She opened her eyes, only a crack, but she managed to look at me. "Thank you, Jonah. Your father would... He is always proud of you."

I didn't know what to say—my throat closed up to the point where I couldn't speak, anyway. I watched as Anissa cleaned the baby as best she could.

"What is it?" Sirene asked.

"A girl," Anissa beamed.

"Is she...?"

"She's wonderful. Just wonderful."

Our eyes met for one brief, silent moment as Anissa worked on the baby and I held on to the mother. Would we ever have this moment ourselves? Would there ever come a time when we could enjoy something as normal as this together?

As normal and spectacular.

My heart went out to my father, knowing he wasn't here to see his child. To congratulate Sirene for a job well done. To whisper words of love to her—yes, love. I could accept the love between them.

They both deserved to have that together.

"You did well," I murmured close to her ear. "He would be proud of you, too."

9

ANISSA

I didn't bother to hold back my tears as I swaddled the baby and placed it on Sirene's chest. A girl. A baby girl.

She was perfect. Beautiful. Her hair, wet and matted, would be red once washed and dried. Just like Philippa's.

She didn't cry, but instead looked around with wide, wise eyes. As though she knew what was happening on some deeper level, beyond us. I wondered if all babies understood better than we thought they did, especially when newborn.

But that could've been the exhaustion, not to mention the mental strain I'd been through.

Which was nothing compared to what Sirene had suffered, of course. Her face was as white as the sheets on which she rested.

"Your baby," I whispered, stroking Sirene's hair. "You made it. I knew you would."

"Thanks to you." Her lips moved, but I barely heard her.

She was still slipping away. I peered down to find fresh blood on the towels under her—granted, it wasn't flowing heavily, but it was still coming out. How much more could she possibly lose without…?

I glanced at Jonah, who'd noticed what I had. His eyes darkened when they met mine.

"Anissa…" I noticed just in time that Sirene was beginning to fade even further, to the point where her arms loosened, and the baby started to slip.

I caught her and handed her off to Jonah, who accepted the little bundle with great care and reverence.

"Stay with us. Stay with us, please. Hang on."

"Take care of the baby…"

"No, no. Please."

She shook her head, eyes barely open. "Hurts."

"I know, but you can get through it." I looked up at Jonah, holding the baby close to his chest. "We have to do something."

"I know. I only wish I knew what."

As did I.

Fane ran through my mind, the way he was hunting for a caster in Duskwood. What would happen after that? Would he come back to the high-rise, searching for Sirene?

Maybe not. I wasn't sure he wanted her to know about his change. But what if he found out she'd had the baby? He'd come back then.

And Jonah would find out about the change, too. And he would know I knew…

I shook my head, pushing those thoughts away. They weren't important right now. The dying woman in front of me was what mattered.

Turning back to her, I leaned closer so she could hear me and I could hear her. "Is there anything I can get you for the pain? Anything that might help you regain your strength?" I didn't know what witches needed or ate but assumed it was the same as humans.

She opened her mouth to speak, but only a tiny mewl of a whimper came out. Fresh tears prickled behind my eyes. This couldn't be happening. She couldn't have fought for so long only to lose the fight. It wasn't fair.

"Would painkillers help you at all?" I asked, my mind whirling. "Human medicine, I mean."

"Where would you get that?" Jonah asked.

"Don't worry about it." I remained focused on Sirene, who barely shrugged.

"Perhaps... but... not enough."

"I know." Whatever I provided would only be a stopgap measure. It was a struggle, keeping my voice gentle and soft for her sake, as hopelessness turned to anger. She didn't deserve to die. "I'll do anything I can right now, and we'll think of something better to do after that. All right? But please, please, just... rest and get your strength back, and don't..." *Die. Don't die, please.*

How could I ever look Fane in the eye if I let her go? I'd already witnessed his heartbreak over Nivia's death, thinking he'd never get Elena back. How much worse would it be now?

My mind made up, I left her so I could wash up in the bathroom adjoining the bedroom. Her blood was all over my hands, under my nails.

Jonah came in as I scrubbed, still holding the baby. "What do you plan on doing?" he whispered.

"Don't worry about it, I told you."

"I hate this. You know I hate it when you take things on yourself and act rashly."

Our eyes met in the mirror, mine flashing anger. "What do you want from me? Do you want me to stand around and let her die in agony? The least I can do is find something to soothe her. If she's going to die, she should at least die in peace."

"You're going to do something dangerous, though. Aren't you?"

"There are levels of danger," I remind him, splashing my face in hopes of cleaning up some of the sweat that had dried there. Every muscle in my body ached horribly, and fatigue had settled into my bones. The last thing I wanted to do was sneak around the city in the dead of night, and he acted as though I was looking forward to the honor.

I turned to him, eyeing Sirene's sleeping form in the next room before continuing. "I have to do something. You wouldn't sit here when you thought you might be able to help, would you?"

"No, I wouldn't."

"So? I don't see the problem. I won't do anything too crazy. You know that by now."

"Do I?" he asked, one eyebrow arched.

"Thanks." I took one more peek at the sleeping baby, who appeared so content in her brother's arms, and made a mental note to get something for her to eat, too. Sirene wouldn't be able to nurse in her condition. I hoped formula would be okay. She was half-witch, too, though. Should I mix blood with it when I gave it to her? Or not? This was all too new to me. I locked eyes with Jonah. "I won't be long. I promise."

"Just come back. That's all I can ask." The baby stirred, and Jonah frowned. "Sooner, rather than later."

"You don't know anything about babies, do you?" I couldn't keep from smiling, though it was a tired smile.

"Why would I?"

"You don't remember when Philippa and Scott were babies?"

"Even if it wasn't hundreds of years ago" —he scowled—

"things weren't the same back then as they are today. Men and boys weren't involved in childcare."

"Understood." I managed to turn away before rolling my eyes. "At any rate, I won't be long if I can help it."

"If you can help it?"

"You know what I mean, Jonah. For now, just do your best with her. I'll bring back supplies."

"Diapers?"

"Yes. Diapers and everything else." It was almost endearing how nervous he was. "Just stay with Sirene and be sure she doesn't need anything. I'm sure water would come in handy right now. She's done so much sweating." And lost so much blood. I left that unsaid, though.

It gave him something to do, at any rate. We went back to Sirene, who was breathing evenly and was blessedly unconscious. Any respite from the pain.

"I'll be back as soon as I can," I whispered, running a hand over her forehead before standing to slide my backpack on. A backpack that had all the tools from a time spent as an assassin and breaking into places, when needing to.

"There's a drug store two blocks down," Jonah murmured as he followed me.

"I know."

"Be careful," he urged before I left. There was no more time to talk over what I was about to do.

I hoped Jonah didn't think the ring on my left hand gave him the right to question every choice I made. He had another think coming if that was the case. As much as I adored him I needed the freedom to make decisions even more. Just when I thought he understood, he'd do something to make me doubt him.

Getting outside in the fresh air was helpful, at least. I could get the aroma of Sirene's blood out of my nose.

Unfortunate that, almost like a bad joke; struggling to deliver a baby while struggling to forget the blood all around me.

I wished I could get to Felicity. She might be able to help Sirene, and she wouldn't care about the witch-vampire complication. At least, I didn't think she would. She didn't seem the type.

There was no time for me to course to Avellane's entrance, though, and there was no telling if I'd be able to find her right away. With her concern about my mother and Allonic, she might be someplace else, and then I'd have nothing to show for all the time I'd wasted in going to get her.

And Sirene would die waiting for me.

I reached the block where the drug store sat and judged the types of foot traffic around it. Pretty light—the clock on the bank across the street read five-thirteen. That explained it. Even New Yorkers had to go to work in the morning, and the bars and pubs had let out already. There was little excuse for the sort of activity I would've found only a couple of hours earlier.

Better for me, of course. I walked around to the alley behind the row of buildings with the hood of my sweatshirt pulled over my head, as always, when I was in the middle of doing something not strictly allowed by law. The drug store was three buildings in—I counted as I walked down the alley, then surveyed the buildings on either side.

Unfortunately, apartments sat on top of each storefront, giving me no option for breaking in through the roof. I couldn't very well cut a hole in someone's bedroom floor.

My next option was to go in through the basement. Luck was on my side, as the double-doored entrance cut into the concrete was only held shut by a rusty old lock. It was nothing to use a pair of cutters, then swing one of the two doors open just enough to slide inside.

There would be an alarm system, wouldn't there? I wouldn't have much time. The basement was dark, but the door leading up to the sales floor was open, and security lights were on there. The light shining down the wooden stairs was enough to guide me through.

I needed all sorts of baby things and had every intention of raiding that aisle, but there was something more pressing. I could always pay for regular baby items. It was the painkillers that I knew I'd never be able to get without the permission of a doctor.

They'd be locked up. Another thing I'd learned from spending so much time in the city, having tuned an ear to the conversations of people on the train I used to take into town when Marcus would send me there, before I had gained the confidence to course out in the open. It had been a real eye-opener, too, the things I used to overhear. These drugs were heavily guarded, for one.

The drugs I wanted ended with "-codone" or "-codeine." I pressed my back against the wall as I slid up the stairs, tiptoe-ing, holding my breath in order to hear any noises coming from elsewhere in the building. It seemed as though I was completely alone. A relief. I still carried weapons in my boots, but it wasn't as though I wanted to use them.

Sirene would hate it if she knew I had killed or hurt someone for her sake.

I walked slowly, carefully, across the floor. If there was an alarm, it wasn't going off as far as I was aware. I knew the alarm could have been silent, but that seemed unlikely. And it would probably be on the front door and windows, going off if somebody broke the glass.

I wasn't about to press my luck. There might be a second

alarm on the drugs, I decided, so I went first for the baby items. My head spun with all the options, but I managed to stuff my backpack with what I guessed were the essentials before zipping up and heading to the back of the store.

Security cameras were likely recording my movements, as best as they could. Vampires move fast, and though I was half-vampire, I was no exception. I rushed through it, moving at vampire speed. Plus, I wore all black, the hood closed tight around my hair and face, my head down as I walked down the aisle and vaulted over the counter.

My heart raced, my palms began to sweat as I scanned the rows and rows of shelves, the names of the different concoctions blurring in front of me. They were all lengthy, unpronounceable, and none looked familiar.

Until I got to a locked case, where boxes of pills sat behind a glass door. There they were. It would take only a few seconds to get back over the counter, then another ten seconds, tops, to get to the door leading to the basement. I could be out of the store in under ten seconds if an alarm sounded when I broke the glass.

For all I knew, there could be someone on the way as I stood there debating my course of action. I needed to get moving.

And so, I used my elbow to shatter the glass case. Right away, a high-pitched beeping sounded. With both hands full of boxes, I took off while without pausing, I shoved the boxes into the deep pockets of my sweatshirt.

Over the counter, down the aisle to the door.

I flew down the stairs and across the basement, my heart thudding like a hammer. For one brief, nightmarish moment, I imagined the doors leading to the alley being locked—or that a police car was waiting there for me. And then what would happen to Sirene and the baby?

I had nothing to fear, as the door opened easily. I made a point of not running but rather walking calmly from the alley and around the corner.

I was already nearly back at the high-rise by the time the lights of three police cars bounced off the building beside me as they sped past.

10

FELICITY

I stepped through the portal and closed it quickly behind me, before anyone could spot the swirling energy field and come looking for the source.

ShadesRealm was just as beautiful and unsettling as I'd found it when we first visited, only the moon was high in the sky at that time of night. A gentle breeze stirred my hair, making my robes flutter slightly. And yet it wasn't the same as the breeze in Avellane. It didn't carry the heavy fragrance of flowers.

The beauty of ShadesRealm was a surface beauty, I recalled as I darted, half-bent, in the direction of a small cluster of trees. I had to find cover before deciding which direction to head in. There was no telling who might be watching.

Where had we come through? I hardly remembered. *Think, think.* I ducked behind the thickest of the trees and leaned against it, catching my breath. The mountains were in front of me but far off in the distance. From where I stood, they were nothing more than foothills. I knew that wasn't truly the case.

Where had they been in relation to me while we were on our way to Tabitha's tower? I closed my eyes, willing myself back to that time. We'd been led and followed by guards, hadn't we? Yes, and the sun had been shining; I'd admired the beauty around me.

And the mountains had been in front of me, to the right. The tower had come up to the left of me after a lot of walking.

I clapped my hand to my forehead, wishing I knew more than I did. I hadn't been in ShadesRealm for more than a few minutes, and already I wondered if I hadn't made a mistake. What did I think I could accomplish this?

I could give Gregor a measure of closure, for one.

And to myself, I could do the same thing. I deserved it just as much as he did, even if the love story I thought I'd shared with Allonic hadn't lasted as long as Gregor and Tabitha's.

If there had ever been love between us at all.

I forced the wistful, somewhat bitter thought from my head as I looked around.

At night, the chances of running into random travelers were less. Wouldn't they be? I had to believe it. I needed some shred of hope to cling to as I gathered my courage and ran from the safety of the trees.

The memory of Garan's veiled warning came back to me. He'd pointed out the woods surrounding the mountains and explained how many bodies were found there all the time, the bodies of those searching for a way into the mountain caves the shades called home.

There had been such foreboding in his words, such coldness. And I had reflected at the time on how there were no hidden dangers in Avellane, that our beauty was true. It didn't mask a rot beneath it.

Was it truly rot, though? Was there something rotten in ShadesRealm? It seemed that way, if women could simply go missing—perhaps be murdered—without so much as an investigation. Garan had been more concerned about Tabitha leaving her tower against orders than about her disappearance.

Did he know about the blood in the tower? I considered this as I ran, scanning the landscape for any sight of the sparkling structure. If he was half the man Gregor was, he would've sent foot soldiers up to the room to investigate. He would know by the time I made my sprint through the tall, moonlit grass something terrible had taken place up there.

Which meant he might have tampered with anything else that could provide a clue.

I stopped, hands on my knees, struggling to catch my breath while I got my bearings. What if I had come out on the opposite side of the mountains? What if I was running in the wrong direction?

I wished there was some other landmark, something I had seen on the first trip that might provide guidance. Unfortunately, the ground was flat, with few trees until one reached the woods which I assumed surrounded the mountains on all sides—a security measure.

I could only keep going until I was certain I'd gotten mixed up, then turn and head back to the trees near where I'd come through and run in the other direction. There would be no shortcuts for me.

I started running again, always looking about me. There was no telling if someone had spotted me—at least the lack of trees nearby meant there was nowhere for a threat to hide. Only the grass which reached my waist. The odds of a shade hiding there were slim. I would spot anyone lying in wait for me.

The sight of the tower rising like a crooked finger in the distance brought tears of relief to my eyes. I put on speed when, only moments before, I'd wanted to lie down in the grass and rest. It felt as though I'd been running forever. Funny, how the sight of one's goal made such fatigue seem insignificant.

Once I was inside the tower, I leaned against the wall and panted. There were still so many stairs to climb, and I was so much more tired than I would've been had I only walked. The ability to course would've come in handy.

I couldn't stop the memory of coursing with Allonic from bubbling to the surface of my thoughts. Tears welled in my eyes, but I knuckled them away with fierce determination. I wouldn't allow myself to dissolve into tears. I had important business to attend to.

And so I began my journey up the endless stairs until I finally reached the top. The air was thinner up here, so far from the ground, and it took an effort to fill my lungs sufficiently.

My heart sank at the sight of the empty room—not empty of possessions, but empty of Allonic. I knew I shouldn't have hoped.

Dried blood still stained the stone floor. I averted my eyes, feeling almost disrespectful by being here. This was where Tabitha had likely breathed her last, and I was intruding. I hadn't even known her.

"I'm sorry, Tabitha," I whispered as I glanced around. The place was still in disarray, as though there had been a fight. Had she struggled? I imagined so, judging by the amount of blood and how it had spread. Who had done this to her?

A glint of metal caught my eye, and I bent to examine the strange looking device on the floor. I turned it in my fingers several times before realizing it was a lock. It had been opened, the hooked piece of metal on top of the barrel swinging freely back and forth.

Why had the lock been used? I hunted for something needing a lock—a chest, a closet, something in which Tabitha would have kept private items. Perhaps someone had been searching through her personal things, and she'd discovered them? It felt like a thin theory, but it was better than nothing.

Even so, I didn't find anything the lock would've been used on. I wanted to throw the thing out the window, angry at its uselessness. At my uselessness.

I stopped myself because doing so would only broadcast my presence in the tower.

What if something in the room had been removed? Anything was possible, I supposed. But what could it have been? What would've been important enough to remove? And who was it being hidden from?

It seemed as though I had uncovered more questions than I'd answered. I hadn't answered any, in fact. Frustration left a sour taste in my mouth as I sat on the modest bed, my head in my hands.

A lock with nothing to lock.

And blood still stained the floor—no one had been in to clean it. Like as not, Garan didn't plan on ever using the tower again. Why would he need to? Its occupant was dead. No longer his problem.

Had he sent someone up here to kill her? The thought chilled me, made me wonder again what I was doing here. He might kill me, too, if he knew I'd trespassed on his land.

Allonic was clearly nowhere nearby. I peered out the window, gazing out in the direction of the mountains beyond the woods.

They found bodies in there all the time, or so Garan had informed me.

But those poor, misguided people hadn't lived in the trees their entire lives. They didn't know how to navigate through thick woods. I did.

Was I insane to consider it? Most likely. But I had nothing to lose, either. I didn't have Allonic anymore. Strangely enough, nothing else seemed to matter very much in light of that development.

I started down the winding staircase which spiraled around the inside of the tower, wondering how many feet had traveled all these hundreds of stairs. How many nights had Tabitha passed, sitting at the window, staring out over the land, thinking of her children and her lost love? Just thinking, unable to do much about anything, unable to take control of her life?

Then again, look at what happened when she had tried to do just that. She hadn't lived long.

Too deep in thought, I barely took notice the shadows spilling across the floor when I reached the bottom of the stairs. Not until I had rounded the doorway and was one short step from leaving the tower.

A pair of hands grabbed my arms and pulled me forward.

"What are you doing here?" asked one of the two soldiers who'd taken hold of me, one on either side.

My heart stopped beating altogether before leaping back into action, racing sickeningly fast.

"Well? He asked a question," snarled the second shade, glaring down at me.

I managed to gasp out an excuse I'd gone over several times during my long run. "I... was hoping to bring back a few of Tabitha's things... to remember her by."

"Where are they, then?"

I should've brought something down with me. "I forgot to

bring anything to carry them in," I lied. "I was going to go back to Avellane and fetch a bag or something."

"A likely story." One of them chuckled and they shared a nasty, knowing laugh.

"It's the truth!"

"Right. You would come all this way, go up all those millions of stairs, just to go back and do it all again." The one who held my left arm leaned down, forcing me to cringe away from him. "You're lying. He doesn't take well to lies."

"No, nor does he take well to trespassers. You were already granted a visit here. Why wasn't that enough for you?"

"I don't know," I whispered, frozen in terror. *Oh, Gregor, I did try. Please, don't come after me. Don't try to save me.* The last thing I wanted was a fight between him and Garan, all because I had been so thoughtless and inexpert.

"Come on."

They dragged me between them, my feet barely touching the ground.

"Where are we going?" I asked, though I knew the answer.

"To Garan," one of them spat. "Where else?"

Where else, indeed.

11

FELICITY

By the time we reached what I assumed was the throne room, I was exhausted and filthy after the long walk through the woods. My robes were caked in dirt and covered in leaves from the few times when I'd stumbled and fallen—the last time, tearing a gash in my knee.

My not-so-very-gallant guides had done little more than haul me to my feet and pull me forward. My arms ached horribly as a result, my knee was swelling under my torn robe, and dried blood covered my lower leg.

I was also frightened out of my mind, with a dozen different arguments racing through my thoughts. Arguments and defenses I hoped would suffice when Garan questioned me.

Even so, I couldn't help but admire what the shades had created millennia earlier. The interior of the mountains had long since been dug out, carved, and smoothed down until an entire underground city had been created. I used to think the feat of ingenuity had led to the City of Trees in which I lived marked the pinnacle of what a creative mind could bring to life. I was wrong.

The room, or cave, in which I stood and waited for Garan to arrive stretched at least fifty feet above my head, and the walls had been painted with images depicting the history of the shades. I recognized the hooded figures, some of them carrying stacks of books and scrolls representing the history they kept for the rest of civilization. The memories they cataloged.

There were mountains and woods, I noted as the soldiers paraded me through the empty cave, and the robed figures who carried their knowledge inside. Behind them was fire, storms, dark clouds. What they had fled—or what had forced them into hiding. I was never quite clear on the history and even had I been, I knew history was written by the victor. There were always at least two sides to a story.

There was no time to examine the rest, as a familiar robed figure emerged from the shadows behind an elaborate throne which seemed to be carved from the mountain rock. He walked with his hands clasped, the sleeves of his golden robe hanging over them. His dark-skinned face was unreadable.

Only the burning of his eyes betrayed his fury. They reminded me of the lit torches lining the walls, doing what they could to illuminate the cavernous space.

"I should've known," he sneered, looking me up and down before shaking his head. "Though I would've thought he was smart enough to send someone less important to him."

"Nobody sent me. I came of my own accord. No one else's."

"Oh, please." He sat with a decisive thump, still sneering. "Spare me your lies. I have little time for them."

"I speak the truth," I insisted, raising my voice so as to mask my fear. I hoped it worked. "He knows nothing about this. Gregor is just as busy as you are, if not more so. He can't waste time on small issues such as this."

"No small issue, and we both know it." He leaned forward, though there was still a great deal of space between us.

He sat above me, at the top of a side set of stairs. He thought himself a king, as Gregor was. Gregor didn't need to seat himself so high above the heads of those he led.

"If this were a small issue—the disappearance of a pathetic vampire-shade atrocity such as Tabitha—he wouldn't have been so adamant in reaching out to me. He wouldn't have taken a chance like that. And he never would've promised me his Knights. We both know it."

I swallowed hard, refusing to give him the satisfaction of watching me crumble under his loathsome stare.

His sneer turned into a smile. "You see the truth of this. I can tell you do. Perhaps you're more intelligent than I gave you credit for—albeit not much more, since you were stupid enough to trespass on our land. You know the punishment."

Did I? I could only imagine he meant to kill me.

"I will, however, show mercy," he continued when I didn't respond, neither in word nor in expression. "You'll find our dungeons more than adequate for someone who's committed as grave a crime as you have."

A dungeon. He intended to lock me up and leave me to rot.

I raised my chin, refusing to let him see me break down. I could do that once I was alone. And I would be alone for a long time, if he had his way. "So be it," I declared. "Do what you will. I only came here to honor Tabitha's memory, to bring back something for Gregor to remember her by. You mock their love, but it was true. I had hoped to do something to ease his pain. I'm sorry you can't understand that. Sorry for you."

His eyes narrowed, his lips pursed. "You have a way with

words. It seems a pity to waste such intellect in our dungeons. I can understand why Gregor kept you by his side for so long."

I inclined my head in acknowledgment of his compliment, as backhanded as it was.

"I'm sure he'll miss your wisdom once the war begins."

My eyes widened before I could keep from reacting. "What do you mean?" I asked, a quiver in my voice.

"Just as I said," he replied, his smile triumphant. "This is exactly the excuse I needed. I suppose I owe you a better fate than the dungeons, but rules are rules. Regardless, you'll be taken care of. Let it never be said I don't know how to repay a favor."

"You can't do this!" I shouted, all pretense of having myself under control falling away as the soldiers began dragging me away.

"But I can!" he called after me in his deep, booming voice. There was laughter in it, and it echoed behind me. "I can, and I will! Thanks to you!"

Thanks to me.

He was going to start a war because of me.

What had I done?

12

ALLONIC

"I'm sorry I was away for so long," I murmured, sitting on a boulder beside the tree. "I needed to spend time with my thoughts and memories. I'm sure you understand."

I raised my chin, looking out over the horizon.

She understood nothing anymore. She never would again. My mother was dead, and it was my fault.

All that was left to remember her by was the mound of dirt beneath her favorite oak tree, a tree we had often sat beneath when I was a child, before she'd been sentenced to life in the tower.

We'd spent endless hours together, observing the clouds as they passed and naming the various flowers and animals who scampered about.

The most precious memories of my life.

She would always be under the tree, with the clouds passing overhead as they once had. When she'd told stories of her life in the human world.

"Do you remember when I used to ask when we'd be able to go to the human world to live together?" I shook my head at my own naïveté. "I never understood the sadness which used to come over you when I'd ask that. I understand it now. I know how much you sacrificed for me. You might have been able to go back there if it hadn't been for me, for wanting to be with me and keep me safe. You could've lived outside that tower. You could've been happy."

And she could've been happy with Gregor, too. They could've built a life together. But not anymore. Because of me. My greed, my stupid lack of vision. I'd only seen what was important to me at the time.

None of it was important anymore. I didn't care about garnering the respect of the shades. I didn't care about taking my rightful place at the top, where I belonged by blood. Look where that ambition had gotten me.

Where it had gotten my mother.

"I hope you like the place I chose for you," I murmured, brushing a few fallen leaves from the mound.

It would settle in time, and grass and flowers would carpet it. Only the stone near which I sat marked the grave. I didn't dare carve anything into it—if Garan found out, he'd have her dug up. I wouldn't put it past him.

I'd spent days in Sorrowswatch after the burial, days which I barely remembered. They'd all blended together, one long stretch of pain and guilt and self-hatred for what I had brought on all our heads. I had destroyed not just her life, but Gregor's. Anissa's. Sara's.

My own.

I stood, staring down once more at the grave. "I've been away too long," I announced. "I should get back to the others and find out if I've missed anything. And if they've missed you. I still don't know what happened to Vance after he did what he did to you. But I promise, I'll find him. And I'll make him pay."

I couldn't be here any longer. I had to go. I turned my back on the grave, my heart tearing to pieces as I thought about her being all alone under the tree for the rest of eternity. She was too beautiful, too good and pure, to be there. Underground. But that was the fate we all shared, no matter how good we were.

Knowing this did nothing to ease my pain. Nothing would.

What would the others think when I returned? I hadn't been to my own chambers under the mountain for more than a few minutes at a time, for longer than I could remember. Ever since Anissa and Jonah had arrived and they'd pulled me into their world.

Did Anissa know? Did Sara? Gregor? What did they think? Were they aware of who had led Tabitha to her murder? I didn't dare go to any of them for fear they were aware and would never forgive me.

What did it matter? I would never forgive myself.

I would miss them, though. Anissa, especially. We had only begun to build a relationship between us. She was always getting herself into trouble, always in need of assistance. What would happen to her without me to call on?

There was nothing I could do about that. She would have to do without me because there was no choice but to remove myself from her life. No matter how it pained me.

After all, I reasoned as walked into the cave and began the journey to my chambers, she might just as easily refuse any assistance I were to offer. And that would pain me worst of all.

"Allonic?" The sound of a familiar voice stopped me in my tracks as I was about to head into my chambers. "Where have you been?"

"Steward." What could I say that would make an acceptable excuse for my long-term absence?

He was rarely anything other than placid, so the sight of his wide eyes and flared nostrils set off warnings in my head. There was something going on which he couldn't wait to share with me.

"Did you hear of the trespasser? Is that why you came back?"

"Trespasser?"

"I suppose not, then," he reasoned, his voice deep and rough as always. "She's been in the dungeon since yesterday. Found at your mother's tower."

My senses went on alert, my skin tingling. "The tower? Who was it?" And did he know of what had occurred in the tower?

"I don't know," he admitted. "There have been so many conflicting reports. None of us can remember a time when a trespasser was jailed. Normally, they lose themselves in the woods, and we find the body later. It's never come to this."

"No. It hasn't."

The dungeons were more a threat than anything, used when one of us committed an infringement. I couldn't remember the last time anyone did. Perhaps that was the sort of thing Ressenden had preferred to keep quiet. I wondered how many other aspects of his leadership he preferred to keep quiet.

He looked around up and down the length of the tunnel we stood in, before continuing. "The reason I felt it important to tell you of this was the girl's description. She has white hair."

My heart sank further than I believed possible. Anissa. What was she doing there?

"She must have lost her mind," I muttered. Searching for me, perhaps? Or for our mother? Yes, and she'd been in the tower.

Once again, someone I cared for was about to pay the price for my selfishness, stupidity, and greed.

"I don't know about that, but I know Garan is furious," Steward reported.

"No doubt."

"He considers this a declaration of war and intends to respond in kind."

"War with the vampires?" I gaped, certain I must have misunderstood him.

Garan was many things, but stupid wasn't one of them. He had no chance of winning a war against a massive vampire army, and their leaders wouldn't be foolish enough to play into his hands. Jonah would never allow it.

Steward frowned. "No, not the vampires. The fae. He's wanted this for a long time, I've heard. An excuse to invade Avellane."

"Avellane?" It felt as though I were trying to hold on to sand with my fingers spread. No matter my intentions, I couldn't manage to make sense of what I'd walked into.

Of course, Gregor would hear of Anissa's capture and, in Garan's mind, this would be enough to warrant a battle.

Was Garan correct about this?

"I have to see him," I decided, pushing my way past Steward in my determination to get to the throne room before Garan did something unforgivable.

"You think he will listen to anything you have to say?"

"I don't know. More than likely, no." I turned down another long tunnel, my rage growing with every step I took.

He didn't know it, but my cousin was about to bear the

brunt of the wrath which had taken root as of late. Losing my mother, losing everyone else I cared about as a result, something had bloomed inside me, something deep and dark and seething.

If he didn't listen, I would find a way to free her.

It was the least I could do.

13

GAGE

"Help..."

Who was that? That pathetic, gasping, whimpering voice? It reminded me of nails running down a chalkboard and sent the same sort of shiver of disgust down my spine. Who was that broken, begging creature?

It couldn't be me.

But I was the only person in the cell. The only person in this entire godforsaken underground pit. Just me. And the rats.

Process of elimination led me to the conclusion it was I who'd whimpered like a broken animal. Whimpered to no one, as there was no one to hear me.

The floor was cold and damp beneath my back. Unforgiving. I'd lost weight, and no longer had the benefit of as much padding between my bones and the harsh surface. I felt every crack, every uneven bit of stone and earth. As though the roughhewn rock beneath me mocked my pain. As though everything around me was part of a great plot to destroy my sanity.

It was working, too. Very well.

I had to stay perfectly still. Every movement was an exercise in agony. Fire flowed through my veins, poured into my muscles, at the merest twitch of a finger or flex of a foot.

Because I was starving.

How long had it been since I last fed? I'd long since lost track. What was the point of counting when there was no end in sight? No end at all? My mind was already beginning to unravel. Why hasten the inevitable?

I'd heard stories of vampires who went without blood for great lengths of time. They hadn't died—at least, not from starvation. Was there dying from starvation for our kind? That would be too easy. No, we probably suffered forever, unless we found another way to end our torment.

Grisly stories ran through my mind, weaving ugly images together which moved back and forth across my consciousness. Taunting me. Foretelling my future. Vampire brethren who had gnawed through their own flesh in an attempt to end the torment. One who had broken free of the dungeon in which he'd been starving and had immediately flung himself from the top of a staircase, cracking his skull open by the time he hit bottom.

But that hadn't been enough. He'd begged one of the others to kill him and end it, and the guard had impaled the wretched, screaming creature on his sword. By then, so the story went, the once-powerful vampire had been nothing but a shrieking wraith. A mere shadow of his former self.

I knew that would be my fate. It was only a matter of time.

Gage...

I closed my eyes, squeezed them tight, refusing to listen to the voice which teased at the edge of my mind. I wouldn't listen. I wouldn't pay attention this time.

Gage... I'm here, my love...

No, no, no, she wasn't here. She'd never be here. Another cruel trick of my fevered, desperate brain. The sound of Cari's voice, calling to me. Whispering promises of solace, comfort, love.

Why won't you look at me...?

"Because you're not here," I whispered. "You're not here. You're not here. Leave me."

But I didn't want her to leave me. I wanted her to stay. I wanted her to help me leave this terrible, hopeless place. This hell.

Worse than hearing her voice was thinking I saw her in front of me, on the other side of the iron bars. She had come after the first few days, and I had never experienced such joy as I did when I first saw her. When I thought I saw her.

The cruelty. I squeezed my hands into fists, barely able to close them.

She wasn't the only one I'd seen, but I'd seen her the most. Jonah had appeared more than once. Fane, only he'd been Dommik again, my father. And I'd seen my mother. What were they trying to do? No, what was my mind trying to do? What was it trying to tell me? Why did it insist on torturing me so?

All of them, bringing up old hurts and slights. Reviewing every shortcoming, every time I had failed. It brought to my memory the early days, when we were all human. The village deacon had told stories of the suffering souls went through before they were clean and whole enough to enter the kingdom of heaven.

Was that what I was going through—rather, putting myself through? Bringing up every single ounce of selfishness I'd ever labored under? Every slight, every sharp word, every mistake? Every time I'd ever been thoughtless and selfish? My soul, or what was left of it, burned with this. All of it. The ultimate cruelty when my body was already wracked with unimaginable pain.

And he knew I was going through it. He knew every single ounce of the suffering he was putting me through.

"Micah." I hated to give voice to his name, hated hearing it echo off the walls and floor and ceiling, quickly fading into the ever-present background noise of dripping water and skittering rat paws.

What was he doing to her? I winced as fire sang through my head when I turned it from one side to the other. What were they doing together? Could I believe she still loved me enough to be true to me? Did I want her to? Selfishly, yes, I wanted her to save herself for me and only me—but there was no chance of our ever being together again. I couldn't ask her to wait forever.

But not him. Anyone but him.

Fresh waves of excruciating pain washed over me, wiping away all thoughts of anything but my physical torment.

Soon, that was all I would be able to think about. The thirst. The hunger. The pain.

I licked my lips to no avail. There was no assuaging the dryness, the ache in every cell of my body. Crying out for the one thing I couldn't possibly have.

Blood. Sweet, hot, thick blood. How had I ever taken it for granted?

Ah, just a drop. Enough to wet the inside of my mouth, to moisten my tongue. I wouldn't ask for more. I wasn't greedy. Just enough to make the thirst go away, to drive away the burning, screaming pain…

The sound of scratching beside my head forced my eyes open.

The rats had grown bolder once it became clear I was no threat. As though their keen instincts understood my weakness. As though they felt me dying. They didn't know I would not die. That I couldn't die, at least, not like this.

And so, they'd begun investigating me. Slowly, taking their time, never behaving too boldly. This one was roughly five or six feet from my face. No more. Far enough it could easily scamper away at the first sign of movement.

I couldn't have caught it if I'd wanted to, my reflexes hopelessly sluggish, and the pain burning through me making it impossible to be sharp or quick.

There was nothing to do but lie here and watch as it assessed me. I didn't dare look away, no matter how I wanted to. Its sleek, black fur, the long tail. The beady eyes, taking me in. Studying me. Who was I, and how much longer until I was dead and ripe for feasting?

The image of a half-mangled corpse with my face turned my stomach. I gagged, bile rising in my throat, my body clenching in agonizing spasms. And still, the rat hovered there, unsure whether to leave me alone or pretend I didn't exist.

And I felt the same about it.

Was it my imagination, or could I hear its heart beating? And the blood flowing from its heart…

"No… no…" I tried to move my arm, to wave it away, and the rat jumped back in response. But it didn't run away. It was bold, it knew I had little strength left. What would happen when they all knew? When I couldn't move without screaming, without my body feeling as though it were being torn into pieces? Would I find the strength to move, to fend them off? Or would I let them do what nature had programmed them to do?

Would it be a mercy?

What if I…

They had blood…

Not much of it…

"No!" I closed my eyes again and kicked out with my feet. That scared it off. I heard its tiny claws scratching against the surface of the floor as it darted off through the crack in the wall, leaving me alone again.

Could I have caught it? Would I have? No.

I wouldn't do it. I wouldn't fall that far. Only mindless, soulless beasts drank the blood of rodents. And that sort of blood did things to a vampire, changed them. I didn't know if it was possible to change back. I didn't want to see for myself, either.

No matter how I suffered, I wouldn't do that to myself.

Would I?

I licked my parched, cracked lips again and wondered. And hoped I wouldn't live long enough to know how far it was possible to fall once true starvation set in.

14

SCOTT

The air didn't move, and yet the fog swirled all around me as I stood not far from where we'd come through.

This was Duskwood. A black, blank sort of place that brought to mind the image of a creator who grew bored with the world they were putting together and deserted it halfway through.

"Come." Fane led the way, my mother's body still resting in his arms.

If it pained him in any way, he didn't reveal it. Only through his hard, intense eyes did I get any sense of what she'd meant to him. That, and how reverently he appeared to carry her.

"What will you do with her?" I asked, careful where I stepped.

I couldn't see the ground. What was down there? The tops of the gravestones just visible over the fog brought to mind another image, more disturbing than the last: hands reaching out from the graves all around me, stretching, seeking something to hold onto as they pulled themselves out.

Or pulled me in.

What was I? A child? I shook off the chilling superstitious thoughts and focused instead on not breaking my neck.

"There are several empty mausoleums here," he murmured.

I noticed the confidence with which he walked. He didn't have to look down, measuring every step. He'd been here many times.

"She can rest in Duskwood until more permanent arrangements can be made. No one here will harm her. That, I'm certain of."

One thing I knew, he would never place her in harm's way. He may have changed in many unimaginable ways, but he loved her.

That brought another question to mind. "I didn't think about this before, but why are we here? If she's... gone... why do we need to find a caster?"

"For Philippa. To take Valerius from Vance's body. Since we have the presence of a necromancer at our disposal, I felt it best not to waste the opportunity. And Valerius must be stopped, by any means necessary."

I couldn't argue the point.

We reached a tall, imposing marble building which I quickly recognized as a mausoleum. A chill ran down my spine. This was where Fane would search for a caster? No great surprise, witches consorting in such a place.

He stepped inside, ducking to clear the low doorway, and placed my mother's body on a low bench while Elazar and I waited.

To his credit, Elazar averted his eyes and seemed to keep a respectful distance. It occurred to me he had just lost someone, too. From the way he'd reacted after finding out she was dead, he had genuinely cared for her.

"Scott? Would you like a minute with her?" Fane beckoned.

I hesitated then shook my head. "I, ah, I already said goodbye to her. A long time ago." I couldn't do it again in front of him, and much less in front of a stranger.

He seemed to understand, or at least to accept my answer, then he led us to another mausoleum. "Hurry. I wouldn't want us to be discovered."

Elazar glanced around with that smirk of his as we hurried through the fog. Did he smirk at everything? I couldn't tell if he actually thought things were funny, or if he thought he was smarter and cleverer than everyone around him and wanted to be sure we knew it, too.

"It isn't much." He ran a hand over the marble face of the wall as we stepped inside. "But even I can admit it's a lot nicer than where I've lived as of late. I would rather never see that place again, if it's all the same."

"I thought you'd want to be there all the time, visiting your sister," I muttered.

He shot me a look of warning, and, for once, the smirk was gone. "Think again, boy."

"All right, all right." Fane stepped between the two of us, doing everything but rolling his eyes. "I thought I left this part of my life behind once my children grew up, but I see that isn't the case."

"It's all right," Elazar assured him with a chuckle. "It's been so long since I've been in the presence of others—save the few visitors I enjoyed over the course of my sentence—I've forgotten my manners. I won't allow my temper to get the better of me."

It was obvious Fane could see right through all of his fake

charm. One thing he still had going for him, he was always a good judge of character.

"Yes, well, you'd better not. I don't think many of the witches who travel through Duskwood would take kindly to your presence here, should you choose to throw a tantrum and run away. Let's not forget the nature of the crimes you committed against them—it takes quite a history of wrongdoing to earn a sentence on Shadowsbane Island."

"And yet your son here almost earned himself a sentence, didn't he? Had my sister not stepped in and altered the course of the—*ahem*—proceedings?"

"And you would still be locked tight in your cell had your sister not freed you. Not only are your crimes notorious, you didn't serve your full sentence."

"Why did you bring me here, then?" Elazar demanded through clenched teeth.

"Because you said you would help," Fane reminded him. "And because if you ever hoped to leave Shadowsbane for any other corner of our world, you'd be hunted and put down like a mad dog. Only my presence is enough to keep you safe right now."

Elazar's eyes reminded me of two burning coals. He didn't have a leg to stand on, no matter how strong and clever he thought he was. And he knew it. "A fair point, well-stated. Your travels through Duskwood should go much better than before, in any case. Seeing as how you've changed."

Fane's eyes widened a millimeter but no more. "Yes, I suppose I should thank you for that." He turned to me, and the tension burst like a bubble. "I'm going to look for a caster willing to help us."

I glanced around, wondering to myself how he planned to find one. "We're not the only people here?"

"Not at all."

"I don't see anyone." I barely saw anything, much less anybody. Only fog which stirred without the help of a breeze, and the tops of tombstones. And the deep, black, endless sky.

"Looks can deceive here," he explained. "It isn't so much a place where witches live as it is a common travel route. A meeting place, as well. There are usually dozens of witches here at one time, but they know how to keep to themselves. As Sirene used the mausoleum to meet others without being noticed, so do the witches who are here now."

"I didn't ask about the habits of witches," I snapped. "I was only questioning how you knew there were others here."

"And I've told you," he replied, raising his chin. "I forget how impatient you can be. And how disinterested in the habits of others. But there's a bit of information I think you need to know, my son. And you are my son, no matter your feelings for me at the moment. I was there the day you were born, and the day you were turned."

Then why have you spent all these years pretending you didn't have children? Why call yourself by another name and insist we use that name when talking about you? Why pretend Dommik is dead?

I couldn't ask any of those questions around Elazar, who stayed silent, but was all ears. Someone who stood as still and silent as he did could only be listening in on the conversation around him.

"What would that be?" I asked, pointedly ignoring Elazar's presence.

"There will come a time when you'll depend on the generosity of someone different from yourself. Perhaps it was wrong of me to allow my children to lead such sheltered lives for so long. The clan was most important, maintaining order and keeping us at peace. I was wrong not to expose you to more of the world—worlds—other than ours. Then again, I knew little of those worlds until we were no longer together, and that was by necessity."

I opened my mouth to speak, but his look brought me to an immediate stop.

His eyes narrowed, fixed on me. "You'd do better to lose some of your hardheaded notions now, before you're at the mercy of one you'd rather not rely on. At the rate you're going, you'll have alienated whoever it is, and there will be no one to help you."

I had quite a lot to say about that, but not where we were or who we were in front of. "Sure. Fine. Do what you have to do. Philippa needs this."

He turned his attention to our companion. Then he strode out among the tombstones and eventually disappeared into the swirling fog which seemed to swallow him. One moment he was there, the next he wasn't. Like magic.

Which it could've been, for all I knew. Stranger things had happened before my very eyes.

Elazar sighed behind me.

I heard him slide down the wall and eventually hit the floor.

He was seated with his back to the wall when I glanced over my shoulder.

"It seems as though there's little for us to do but wait," he observed.

"It seems that way." The less I said to him, the better.

He'd find a way into my head if I wasn't careful. No one had to explain it for me to know it was true.

"You've been here before?"

It seemed an innocent question. "No. This is my first visit."

"Hmm." Nothing more than that.

"What's so strange about my never being here before?"

"Nothing. It makes sense, if you're as sheltered as your father said."

"I wouldn't call myself sheltered."

"Who would?" he chuckled. "Please, don't misunderstand me. I don't mean to be insulting."

"Oh, I'm sure you would never want to insult anyone…"

"It was merely an observation. And, really, isn't it every parent's instinct to protect their child? After all, your father hid himself from you for decades in order to protect you."

Damn him. Just when I'd sworn to myself I wouldn't let him in my head. "How would you know about that, locked up the way you were?"

"Word has a way of spreading, even behind invisible bars," he explained. "Your father is a very well-known personality—regardless of the name he uses. In fact, he garnered more fame for himself as Fane than he ever did as Dommik—"

"Don't say his name," I warned.

He didn't deserve to speak the name of my father. I didn't care how it looked, my snapping at him that way.

He only snorted softly. "A thousand pardons. I meant no disrespect."

"It seems as though you manage to say a great many disrespectful things without the intention of disrespect."

"Always my curse." He chuckled. "I have a way with words. Not a good way, mind you."

I glanced away again, over the tombstones. So many of them. Ancient. There was no telling just how ancient they were. I wondered if he would know but wasn't in the mood for the mental gymnastics it took to have a simple conversation with him.

Be that as it may, the only alternative was to hang around in silence. I could've handled the silence under ordinary circumstances, but when surrounded by pressing blackness and the sense the fog swirled without the air stirring it...

"What did you do?" I glanced over my shoulder.

"To be locked away?"

"Yes. Fane alluded to crimes you committed. How serious they were. I think it would be nice to know who I'm dealing with if we're going to be traveling together."

He surprised me by laughing. "I've never been able to stand down in the face of reason. Let that be known as one of my better qualities, since I know my lesser qualities are what will be remembered long after I'm gone."

"I'll be sure to spread the word." I turned away from the landscape outside the mausoleum, facing him with my back to the wall.

"Are you sure you want to hear what I have to share?" He raised an eyebrow in challenge. "They're not pretty stories."

"Don't buy into Fane's version of me," I warned. "He's been away for a long time. A lot of water has passed under the bridge since then."

"Oh, I've seen what you're capable of. You're no child," he observed with an arch grin.

I wasn't sure if he was making fun of the scene I'd caused on Shadowsbane or expressing approval. Maybe both. If anything, it led to him being freed. He had no room to mock me.

"So? Are you going to tell me, or not?"

"Why is it so important you hear what I've done?"

I shrugged. "I thought it would be something to pass the time. A diversion. What's the alternative? Waiting for Fane and a caster until we both rot? Hanging around, thinking about who we've lost?"

Just like that, his genteel, charming façade shattered. "What do you know about loss, boy? You've lost nothing."

That threw me; the last thing I'd expected was for him to turn on me like that. "You were there. You saw what happened. And I saw what happened to you."

"You know nothing of loss," he hissed, his voice reminding me of a snake's. Somehow, it was much more chilling than a shout or scream. "You don't know what it is to love another, to devote yourself to them body and soul. You don't know what it means to share a life with another, to truly share. Even when one of you is taken away, locked up, and the other remains faithful to you for all that time. When they give up everything to be with you, just to be with you, because you both know there's no life without the other. To take strength and courage from the presence of that other half of yourself, to live for the moments in which you're together—even if you can't touch each other."

He looked away from me, staring at the wall opposite the one against which he sat. Staring through it, seeing something far away. "I didn't get to touch her again until she was already gone. Cold and dead. How cruelly fate can twist sometimes. I lived for the moment I could touch her again, I truly did. There were days when that one fantasy was all that got me through without losing my mind. And yet..."

The depth of his reaction stunned me into silence. It was the last thing I'd expected to hear from someone like him. To think he'd truly felt for Samara.

"And you believe you've lost something," he mused, tipping his head back against the wall with a sigh. "It would be laughable if it weren't so tragic. So misdirected. You lost nothing in that little girl. She never loved you."

"You know nothing," I growled, fangs ready to descend. The only thing that stopped me from throwing myself onto him and tearing him to pieces was the thought of Philippa, and how she needed him. Nevertheless, I wondered what it would be like to bathe in his blood.

"I know much more than you do," he whispered. "If the girl had loved you—really loved you, ready and willing to join her life to yours—she wouldn't have had her head turned by Stark or any other. You don't think someone as beautiful as my Samara had her share of chances to fall into another's arms? You don't believe there were times when she felt lonely, hopeless? With hundreds of years stretching out in front of her, standing between us?"

"That doesn't mean there was nothing between us, or that I don't feel her loss keenly."

"It would be better for you to forget she ever lived," he advised with a grim smile.

"I would love nothing more than to be able to do that."

"Do it, then. It's not as difficult as you want to believe it is."

"How? If you're so experienced, how would I go about forgetting her?"

"See a little more of the world, of life," he suggested. "I realize they who live in Manhattan believe it's the center of the universe, but I can assure you that isn't so. You've seen nothing, you've experienced nothing. You throw yourself around like a spoiled child—"

That was enough for me. I couldn't have cared less if Philippa or Vance or anybody else needed him.

A single snarl escaped from my throat before my fangs descended and I threw myself across the mausoleum, claws extended and ready to rip him apart.

He didn't flinch. He merely waved a hand in my direction and sent me sprawling.

It was like hitting a wall of solid energy. There was no fighting something like that. I hit the floor with a bone-crunching thud and saw stars for a moment before shaking my head to clear it.

"Now. Have you gotten that out of your system?" He sounded bored. He actually sounded bored.

"You bastard."

"Words, words, words." He sighed. "They mean nothing to me by now. I've been called just about everything under the sun. I believe new epithets have been invented in my honor. None of them mean a thing, not really. I know who I am and what I am, and that's all that's ever mattered."

I was still too stunned to speak. He took advantage of my silence.

"If you'd like to hear a story or two, I would be happy to share. But you must promise to keep your naïve, inexperienced mouth shut. I don't care how old you truly are. You might as well be a babe in the woods."

I rankled at his insulting words and tone but wasn't stupid enough to argue.

My curiosity was stronger than my pride.

15

SCOTT

Elazar drew a deep breath and seemed to settle himself in, as though he'd been waiting for this opportunity.

I was a captive audience, after all, and he'd had a lot of time to go over his memories, but no one new to share them with it seemed.

"If anything, I must admit there's not much I could've done without Samara's assistance," he began. "Not that I blame her for anything which took place once the Senate captured me. It took the two of us, with our abilities combined, to perform the feats we were so renowned for. I knew from a young age who I was, what I was," he continued, staring into space as he had before. "I was hardly looked on favorably once my abilities revealed themselves, to put it mildly. No matter the creature, no matter how reviled or excluded they might be in the eyes of others, they were always searching for someone to look down upon. One would think they'd be more likely to accept others, wouldn't you think?"

He didn't wait for me to answer.

"My mother was an elemental witch, as my sister is. Possibly one of the most misunderstood of our kind. I was once naïve enough to believe she would be capable of relating to me as a result of this. Not so. She threatened to banish me. I disgusted her. But not Elewyn; she loved me, always, and was always faithful to me. She urged our mother to at least allow me to remain under her roof and her protection. And Elewyn was a rising star, possessed of skill even our powerful mother revered. She may as well have hung the moon and stars, that girl."

I didn't so much as raise a brow. I did nothing that would interfere with his storytelling.

He chuckled fondly. "There was never any rivalry between us. We were both powerful in our own way and content to leave it at that. She expressed concern when I began taking my skills... public, shall we say. When those aware of my powers came to me with questions about loved ones who had already passed through the veil between life and death, my reputation grew quickly.

"Elewyn wanted me to exercise more caution. She wanted me to tamp down the full depth of my power, but there was no controlling it. Nor did I want to. I'd spent more than enough time denying myself for the sake of sheer survival in my family. No more."

"What did you do?" I asked.

He shrugged. "I brought my mother's greatest rival back from the dead and used the reanimated corpse as a weapon against her. Mother didn't last long, even with all her considerable power. You see, it was she who had killed the unfortunate witch in the first place. She didn't think we knew. That was her mistake—one of many."

My stomach turned. The way he spoke of it, so matter-of-fact, as though he were reporting the weather.

"I quickly grew tired of reanimating the dead, however. A messy business. Enough to turn even the strongest stomach. No, it was much cleaner and more interesting to transport spirits from one body to another. When I met Samara, I knew I had found my purpose. I couldn't begin to tell you how many we assisted this way."

"Assisted?" I spat.

"Yes. Assisted. You know—the way we assisted Nivia and Valerius."

"It's disgusting, what you did."

"In your eyes. Not in theirs. They needed us. We provided a service."

"I'm glad you can explain it to yourself that way. It must make being you a lot easier."

He laughed, the sound falling flat as the sound did, rather than echoing off the marble walls. "It does, in fact. But, as you know, the Senate felt much the same about my services as you do. They caught up to us and felt it best to sentence me."

Something about that didn't add up. "What about Samara? Why did only you receive a sentence, when it took the both of you to do what you did?"

He didn't answer right away, but the shadow of emotion which seemed to move over his face confirmed my suspicions. He had taken the blame for all of it because he'd loved her. "It wasn't difficult for me to convince the Senate I'd held Samara under a sort of thrall, forcing her to do what she'd done. Necromancers are so detested, and the Senate wanted so badly to punish me until the end of time, they were eager to believe whatever it took in order to justify their sentence."

He rolled his head on his shoulders, his eyes boring into mine. "You see what I mean, now? She could've left me, taken her lucky break and run. Instead, she moved her life to Shadowsbane and lived in the shadow of that prison until the day she..."

His voice left me cold and shaken to my core. The images his story had brought to mind. The recognition that he was right, that Sara had never loved me enough to make such a sacrifice for me though I would've done what Elazar did for Samara, if it would've meant her freedom.

She had come to me at a terrible time, a time of weakness and fear. She'd needed someone with strength, stability, the promise of comfort after the torture she'd been through. I had been there for her, and available. It was all she'd needed.

When she'd no longer needed me, she'd moved on. And changed. Had she ever changed?

I was better off without her. Just listening to the stories of Elazar's life, his history, proved I was right about witches and their ilk. Evil, nasty, heartless things. Capable of the vilest aberrations. His mother, an elemental witch like Sara, had murdered her rival. What would Sara be capable of?

I didn't want to know.

We didn't hear the footsteps until Fane, and the small, black-haired witch who followed him were almost inside the mausoleum.

I jumped to my feet. "That didn't take very long."

"I was fortunate." Fane glanced at Elazar, who stood and looked the witch up and down. "This is Branwen. She is a caster, and she's agreed to assist us."

She was slight, delicate, with large eyes that seemed to take up most of her face. Her robes were long, deep burgundy, swallowing her tiny body. I had to remind myself of how dangerous she was—it would be too easy to underestimate her.

"I'm glad to meet you." Elazar smiled.

Her still expression didn't shift an inch. "I'm well

acquainted with you, Elazar. I'm not one for false compliments, so you will forgive me if I don't return the warmth of your greeting."

I almost laughed at the way Elazar's face fell. He hadn't been expecting that, the fool.

Fane cleared his throat, stifling a smile of his own. "Branwen is an old friend of Sirene's—it's only fair I tell you the strength of their friendship is the reason she's agreed to help us, and nothing more."

"I know Sirene would want me to assist you," she added, never taking her eyes from Fane. "And now that you are one of us, it becomes easier for me to fulfill her wishes."

I glanced at Fane in surprise, only to find him appearing just as surprised as me.

"One of you?" he choked out.

"Well, yes. The change in your aura is obvious. You're now a warlock. Is that not so?"

He looked at Elazar, who was all innocence. "Yes," he replied, his jaw tightening until muscles jumped there. "That is so. It's a rather recent occurrence, not one I've had time to grow accustomed to yet."

Disgust threatened to choke me again. My father, a warlock. Because of the evil necromancer, I still wanted nothing more than to kill someone. Slowly.

"And you."

I realized she was speaking to me. Our eyes met. She seemed to stare through me—an unnerving experience.

"Me?"

"You're very angry, aren't you? I sense a great deal of turmoil in you."

"And?" I challenged.

Fane's disapproving sigh only made me grit my teeth.

She chuckled softly, never breaking the hold of her gaze

on mine. "If I can't trust you to behave yourself, I don't know that I'll be able to help you."

"You're having a little fun with me, aren't you?"

"Perhaps."

"I don't appreciate it."

She tilted her head to the side. "I don't recall asking whether or not you did."

I growled under my breath. "No filthy witch talks to me that way."

Just like that, the air left my lungs as though an invisible iron band wrapped itself around my midsection. I couldn't breathe, much less speak, no matter how hard I tried.

She only glared as her spell or whatever it was took control of me. "I think it would be best for you to recall who's truly in power here, bloodsucker. You need your fangs in order to work your will on others. I don't need to touch you or even lift a finger to steal the air from your very lungs."

"Branwen. Please." Fane touched her shoulder as I struggled for air, doing everything I could to keep from making my struggle visible.

It grew more difficult by the second.

And then, just as immediately as it had come on, the hold she had on me disappeared, and I could breathe again.

I glared at her as I caught my breath.

Fane pulled me aside. "Are you all right?"

"Fine," I replied. "She's really something. You run in all the right circles, don't you?"

"Watch what you say," he snarled. "I've about had my fill of your attitude and your inability to control it and your mouth. No matter how many times I remind you how important it is to Philippa that we make a success of this, you insist on making a fool of yourself."

"Why did you bring me along, then? You could've let me go home, and everything would've been fine."

He sighed. "I thought this would be different. I was wrong. I also thought you would've learned your lesson by now, based on what happened back on Shadowsbane. What needs to happen for you to finally understand how wrong you are about so many things? You can't keep allowing this ignorance and anger to rule you, or the time will come when I won't be there to help get you out of the hole you've dug for yourself. No one will."

He didn't understand and never would. He was one of them. It felt as though we were speaking two different languages, just missing one another. And there would never be time for us to arrive at an understanding, because there would always be some new challenge or danger to focus on.

There would never be time for us to get back what we'd lost.

When I didn't answer, he went on. "This is important for Philippa. Can you remember that, at least?"

"Yes, of course."

"I need to know you're going to hold your tongue and behave for her sake, if for nothing else."

Right, because he cared so much for his little girl. She'd always been his favorite. I hated myself for caring so much, for begrudging my sister her happiness, but it didn't help at the moment that he cared so much more for her happiness than my misery.

"I will," I promised, swallowing my resentment. "Really. I'll be all right. We should get going, this place unnerves me."

He chuckled. "We can agree on that, at least. I've never quite gotten used to this world."

16

PHILIPPA

Having Vance back was a dream come true. Something I had wished for, worked for, put all my hopes into. I didn't think I had ever wanted anything more, not even back when I was a little girl, and the entire world had been made up of nothing but me and what I wanted.

I should've been happy.

I wasn't.

And I didn't know what to think.

What was worse than anything was the way he didn't seem to notice. Or care. Didn't he know me at all? I thought he did. There was a time when we were closer than any two people had ever been, or so I used to tell myself.

He had always been able to pick up on my slightest change before. I used to have to tell him to stop watching my face, because every time I'd have a thought that made me frown, he'd think I was frowning at him. Vance had a lot of shortcomings, but attentiveness was never one of them.

Had he changed so much in the time we were apart?

I guessed it was possible. It had been forever since we'd

been together, and that amount of time could change anyone. I had mellowed out a lot since those days. Even more in the short time since we'd met Anissa and Sara, I had grown a lot. Not that it helped me dislike them any less.

That had to be why he was so different. That, and how much he'd been through when Valerius took over his body. I had no idea what that was like and knew I'd never understand even if Vance tried to explain it.

Why was his kiss so different, though? Wasn't that something that shouldn't have changed? Why would it have? A kiss was something unique to each person. It didn't change just because time had passed. Did it? It was almost like...

Like he wasn't there.

No. That wasn't possible. I had spoken to Valerius while he was in Vance's body. I remembered it. That was nothing like this. He was a completely different person.

Wasn't he?

"Are you all right?" I asked when I found him staring out the window.

He seemed so tense, with his shoulders up around his ears and his hands clasped behind his back.

Nothing.

"Vance?" I crossed the living room, almost afraid to startle him.

He'd been through so much already. He must not have noticed my reflection in the door, because when I touched his back, he whirled on me like he'd turn on an attacker.

I jumped back, pulling my hand away.

For a split second, no longer than the blink of an eye, he looked like a different person. His features were his, but they weren't. There was something wrong with the way he held his face. He was harder, angry, even violent.

And then, he wasn't.

VINDICATION

"I'm sorry," he murmured, hands held up with the palms facing out. "I didn't mean to scare you."

When I found my breath, I said, "I didn't mean to startle you either. I'm sorry."

More than anything, I was confused. Would he always be this way? Was I supposed to get used to him being so jumpy, so unpredictable? So not him?

"I was a little too deep in thought," he explained, giving me that Vance shrug I knew so well. That tiny gesture I had seen so many times went a long way toward soothing me.

"You don't have to think about any of those things anymore if you don't want to. You can leave it in the past now. I hope you know that." I slid my arms around his waist as I spoke, just for the joy of touching him. I was so sure for so long I never would again—and for even longer than I would never want to again—that I couldn't get enough.

"That's an easy thing to say when you haven't killed your own father."

"That wasn't you," I whispered, pulling him a little closer. "I wish you could forgive yourself."

"You and me both." He chuckled. His eyes were so troubled, so much older than they used to be.

I wanted to wipe all of that away and bring him back to what mattered. Would that ever be possible?

"You know," he continued with a frown, "there's still something you haven't told me, though I've asked. I feel as though you're trying to keep something from me."

Talk about feeling like a deer in headlights. I blinked slowly before asking, "What is it?"

"Where is the body? Valerius's body?"

Another blink as my thoughts spun around in circles. "I don't understand the obsession with where his body is. I'm telling you, it's safe. There's absolutely no reason to worry about it."

"Valerius had to go somewhere when he left me, right? He could be walking the earth, back in his own body."

"You saw his body," I reminded him. "I don't think he's walking anywhere."

He frowned, and again, for around the length of the blink of an eye, he was someone else. His nostrils flared, his eyes narrowed, one corner of his mouth curled into a sneer. As though there was still a piece of the evil, ancient one in there, wanting to lash out at me for insulting him.

"He's pretty powerful," Vance pointed out, calming down again. "I wouldn't put anything past him. I hate to think of you going to check on him and him…"

He had a point. Where had Valerius's—was it his soul—gone? He could be anywhere. I wished there was someone I could talk to about it, but who would have experience with something like this?

There was no one to help me. Not even anyone from my family. I had never felt so alone, not ever. I was all alone, handling everything that everybody else used to think was important.

And I had done well so far. I could do well with this.

For starters… "Considering where he is, I know he's all right. Completely safe."

"You can't know that."

"I do. Just trust me. You have to."

"Why do I have to? Why can't I see for myself?" He pulled away, taking a few steps back. "Why are you keeping this from me?"

"Honestly?"

"Yes, please."

I braced myself for what might happen. "Because it seems

like you care too much. I don't understand why my word isn't enough."

He snorted. "Because you haven't always been the most responsible person in the world, Philippa. I think we both know this."

I winced. I wanted to slap him. I wanted to cry. He had never insulted me like this before—he was always completely aware of his faults and never tried to pretend to be someone he wasn't. Which meant he never dug at the faults of others. Especially not mine, not even when things had been at their worst between us.

"You don't know what you're saying right now."

"I don't? It seems to me that I do. I'm sorry if things that happened in the past leave me worried about your level of responsibility, but there you are. I can't help what's happened in the past, can I?"

"Neither can I!" I shouted. "But you're speaking to me now like I'm a child, which I most certainly am not." All the same, I started to question myself. I hadn't checked on Valerius all day, had I?

No, I hadn't. I was going to before Vance showed up at the front door. What if something happened to him? What if he was down there, in the vault, awake and waiting to attack when I came in?

Then why would I want to go to the vault at all—without backup, at least?

Vance knew how to drive the knife in and turn it, calling up all my old insecurities. All the things I wished I had never shared with him. The exclusion I used to feel when my father would only talk about clan-related business with my brothers. The way I'd decided to play the role of carefree party girl because it was what they expected of me. It all came rushing back, thanks to him.

"Why are you doing this? Why are we doing this?" I asked, throwing my hands into the air. "I just got you back and look where we are. It's time for us to focus on what's important; and this isn't important."

"Maybe not to you," he spat. "It is to me. Something else you never managed to learn."

I gaped at him in wonder. How could he turn on me so quickly? "I need to not see you for a minute," I whispered, turning to go to my room.

"Don't bother. I need some air." He went to the door, and I noticed the way he'd clenched his fists as they swung by his side.

"Where are you going?"

He only scoffed, barely glancing over his shoulder. "Don't worry about it. I've been taking care of myself for a long time —and there's nothing you could do to help me." The door slammed shut behind him.

I let out a sharp gust of air, leaning against the wall as my legs went weak. What was that about? What happened to him? Was he always going to be this way, like two sides of the same coin? Would being with him mean always wondering which side was about to face up?

I jumped, squeaking out a gasp of surprise when the door to the balcony opened.

My fangs descended before I recognized the tall figure of the man who stepped through. Dark hair blew around his face before the door closed again leaving the wind outside.

"Dad—I mean, Fane." It came out as a sigh of relief. Finally, somebody was there who might help me understand what was happening.

At least, I thought so until I noticed the change in him. It was subtle, nothing I could put my finger on right away. He was himself... but not himself. How was that possible? "What happened to you? Something's different. Where have you been?"

"Since when do you ask so many questions?"

"Since when do you answer a question with a question?"

He opened his mouth to throw back a response, but nothing came out. "*Touché*," he murmured with a half-smile. "My clever girl. You haven't changed."

For one brief moment, things were the way they used to be. There was no stretch of empty time between us, no lost past. I had forgotten how much we needed him. No matter how strong a leader Jonah was, our father would always be the rock of the family.

Even if there was something very strange about him. Something off.

He jerked his head toward the glass doors. "I've been waiting out there until you were alone."

I wrapped my arms around my waist. "How long were you out there?" I asked, more than a little unnerved to know he was watching. Listening.

"Long enough to know you know something is wrong. You do, don't you?" He looked at me with a mixture of concern and pity. If it had come from anyone else in the universe, I would've lashed out and sworn I didn't need either from anyone.

Coming from him, I felt relief. "You saw it, too?"

"Of course. Because that isn't Vance."

"No. That's not true. You don't know what you're saying." I shook my head, backing away, like that would distance me from the bitter truth of his words.

He sighed. "Philippa, please. Think about it. You saw and heard how different he is."

"How could you possibly hear what was happening in here? Even if you had your ear pressed to the glass..."

"I didn't need to. I could watch your body language together. I saw how his words hurt and stung." He held out his hands, reaching for me. "Philippa, if Vance was really back with you, after having been through so much, do you think he would hurt you that way?"

My chest clenched in recognition of this, since I had been asking myself those very questions. Why was he acting so unlike himself?

"He's changed a little, is all," I insisted. "He's been through so much."

"Why are you so determined to believe him?"

"Because it's better than the alternative. Knowing he fooled me." I turned away, my hands over my face. It was true. It had to be. I only wanted Vance to come back to me, wanted it badly enough to ignore everything different about him. I had willfully led myself into being hurt, all because I was so determined to have Vance back.

"I'm sorry. I'm so sorry." He wrapped his hands around my upper arms and turned me to face him.

Before I knew it, I was against his chest and sobbing my heart out. A little girl all over again. The relief of being there, held by my father, made the tears flow harder than before.

"I... oh, I'm so disgusted," I sobbed. "I kissed him... and..."

"You love him. Of course, you did," he murmured, stroking my hair. The sweet moment didn't last long, however, before he stiffened and pulled back. "We don't have much time. He'll be back soon. He hasn't gotten what he wants yet."

Naturally. "The body," I whispered, still crying. "That's why he wants it. He wants to get back into it."

"Right. And it is...?"

"Still in the vault. I've been keeping watch on it all along."

"Good." He looked at the door, as though he were waiting for Vance—no, Valerius—to come bursting in. "You're going to pretend to believe him when he comes back."

"What?"

He nodded, glancing out toward the balcony. "I'm not alone. Scott is with me, and a couple of others."

"Scott's out there?"

"Yes, and others who can help us."

"With what?"

"Putting Valerius back into his body so you can have Vance back. The real Vance."

My heart soared when I realized he was there for me. My happiness. But... "Why would we need any help with that? He wants to get back into the body. Otherwise, why would he be so intent on finding out where it is?"

"Think about it. Why would he want to possess that old, decaying body again when he could stay in Vance's young, healthy body?"

The realization sent a cold chill through me. "He only wants to know where it is so he can protect it, keep watch on it. Make sure no one harms it."

"Precisely. He wouldn't go back willingly—at least, I'm betting on it. We'll have to do it for him."

"Who will?"

"You'll see." He hurried to the glass doors. "Remember: when he comes back, we never had this conversation, and you have no idea he isn't really Vance. Apologize if you have to. Whatever it takes. But be sure not to overplay your hand, either. He'll be wary, ready to pounce on the slightest indication you've changed your mind too quickly. You're going to offer to show him the body."

"And then what?"

"Take him down to the vault. We'll take care of the rest." He opened the door, ready to step outside.

"Fane. I... —"

"There's no time," he whispered, eyes on the front door. "Just remember not to give yourself away. Don't be too eager to get down there."

"All right."

I wanted to thank him for what he was about to do, whatever it was. I wanted to apologize for anything I might have said or done when he first came back that might have given him the idea I wasn't happy to have him in my life again. It would have to wait.

Once he was outside again, I rinsed my tear-streaked face at the sink in the bathroom Valerius had used for his shower. Would it be possible to burn the entire room down but leave the rest of the penthouse unscathed? To think, I had let him touch me. I had let him... —

The hinges squeaked as the door to my place swung open.

I looked at myself in the mirror over the sink, willing myself to play my part. I was used to pretending to feel differently than I did, wasn't I? I'd been doing it for most of my life.

For once, Valerius was about to find out he wasn't the cleverest one in the room.

17

ANISSA

"I'm back," I breathed, almost laughing as I hurried into the penthouse with my bulging backpack. "I can't imagine how many laws I just broke. Human laws, I mean." Adrenaline poured through me—no matter how accustomed I was to slipping in and out of otherwise locked buildings, it never ceased to excite me.

Jonah held a finger to his lips as he paced the floor, holding the baby the way a man would hold a live bomb he was afraid might explode at any second.

And he held a bag of blood in one hand.

"What do you think you're doing?" I whispered, frozen in a mix of horror and amusement.

"Getting ready to feed the baby," he replied, as though I was asking the stupidest question he'd ever heard. "We always keep the refrigerators stocked with at least one bag, even in these unused apartments. Just in case. I'm glad I remembered."

"That's good to know," I murmured, approaching slowly so as not to wake the baby. "But babies need more than blood. In fact, I imagine that's the last thing this baby needs."

I'd been thinking about this the last few minutes and had come to a pretty reasonable conclusion. At least, I thought I had.

"How would you know?"

I shrugged.

"Oh." He looked like a little boy whose balloon was just busted.

"You didn't know." Plus, I could be wrong... "First, even more important." I pulled out a pack of diapers, wipes, and cream from my backpack and brought them to the sofa. He watched in awe as I fumbled my way through diapering a newborn. This, I had never done.

At one point, our eyes met, and we both smiled. How surreal, doing this together. It felt for a second as though she was ours. We had brought her into the world together, after all. No matter where I went after this, I'd always feel a connection to this sweet, squirming little baby who gazed up at the two of us with her wide, innocent eyes.

After she was swaddled up again—we needed clothes, and I'd probably have to actually purchase them in a store versus stealing them—I waved him into the kitchen, which was essentially a smaller version of the one upstairs. Very modern, very sleek. It seemed a waste, though. Why have a beautiful kitchen when vampires didn't eat food? And only vampires lived here.

One of many questions I had never thought to ask and didn't have the time to think about right now. Not when a baby needed to eat.

I pulled out a can of formula and a pack of bottles. "They only had powdered formula back when Sara was a baby," I explained, rolling up my sleeves and washing my hands before washing one of the bottles. "Things have come a long way."

"You're not that much older than her, are you?"

"Old enough to remember. And I was at the age where a kid wants to be helpful," I smiled, remembering the way I'd insisted on helping make up Sara's bottles, then insisting on being the one to feed her. I followed the instructions on the side of the can and poured out a couple of ounces.

"That's it?"

"I think so." I held out the bottle, smiling hopefully. "Do you want to do the honors?"

"Oh. I don't know." He winced, looking down at her like he'd never seen a baby before. "Should I? Maybe you should; you've done it before."

"There's nothing to it." I had to turn my back on him or else risk Jonah seeing me struggling not to laugh.

There he was, the leader of a clan. The leader of all the clans, for the time being. Smart, trusted, wise. And terrified of giving a baby a bottle.

I led him to the sofa and handed him the bottle once he sat down, then wedged a pillow under his arm. "Here. Be comfortable."

It was a joy to watch him cautiously guide the bottle into the baby's mouth. She opened her eyes and gazed up at him.

That was it. He was hooked.

An expression came over his face that I'd never seen, even when he looked at me. Awe was the closest thing I could come to when trying to decide what it reminded me of. She'd always have a protector in her big brother.

"You're a natural," I whispered, smiling as he grinned.

"Do you ever think about this? For us, I mean?" He managed to pry his eyes from his new best friend long enough to look my way.

"Of course. All the time," I admitted. "When I'm not thinking about necromancers and elemental witches and…"

"Understood." He chuckled. "So do I, in case you ever wondered."

"I guess we should get through the wedding, first." A wave of sadness washed over me as I thought about my mother not being there. I tried to push it away so he wouldn't see it.

"Why not? They didn't wait," he pointed out, referring to Fane and Sirene.

"What can I say? I'm an old-fashioned vampire-fae hybrid."

Once feeding time was over and we fashioned a makeshift bed for the baby out of blankets and pillows, I went to check on Sirene. She was smiling in her sleep, even though every breath sounded like she was underwater.

"She may have bleeding inside," I murmured when Jonah joined me. "There was so much trauma. Pushing the baby out for her and everything."

"I did this?" he asked, staring at her.

"No, I didn't mean that. It's just a fact. No wonder they say this is so dangerous for witches. I can't believe she survived it."

"But I did," came the whisper from the bed.

I gasped, embarrassed, as her eyes fluttered open. I didn't know she could hear me.

"I'm sorry if we woke you," I murmured as I went to her side. "I didn't want to. I only wanted to check on you."

"To see if I was still alive?" She was barely smiling. "I understand."

"I brought something for you." I emptied my pockets onto the bed, boxes spilling everywhere.

"Anissa? Were you trying to get arrested?" Jonah asked as he looked over my haul.

"I didn't know how much we'd need, and I wanted to help Sirene with the pain." I picked a box at random, opened it and read the directions. "Sirene, do you think it's all right if you take one of these? It won't hurt you, will it?"

"I don't think so. We prefer more natural means, of course, but I'm in no position to be choosy."

Jonah helped her sit up enough to swallow two pills with a sip of water. She rested with a sigh, exhausted from the small bit of movement.

"At least you won't hurt anymore," I whispered as I stroked her hair, wishing there was something else I could do. As always.

"Where's the baby?" she asked, eyes already closing again.

"Sleeping. Fed, diapered, contented."

"That's good. I knew I was leaving her in good hands..." She was asleep again.

I met Jonah's worried gaze. He motioned for me to join him in the hall.

"We have to get a witch for her," he fretted when we were alone.

"She's still talking like she's going to die."

Just putting it into words turned my heart heavy. She expected to die. She seemed ready to go, even. Resigned. It might have seemed like a better alternative to the pain she was living in.

"I know," he whispered, wrapping me in a tight hug. "Which is why I want to do something to make it not turn out that way. Would you be all right with me leaving you alone with the baby?"

"If it means finding someone to help us, yes. Of course." I pulled back, searching his face for confirmation. "What are you thinking?"

"I wish I knew. If I could only find Fane. He'd know what to do. Otherwise, I've been wracking my brain, but I'm coming up with nothing. Where's Allonic? Do you know? He could create a portal."

I sighed. "I don't know, and it's bothering me. I haven't seen him for far too long, now. He could've stopped in upstairs, looking for me." I wanted to talk to him about our mother. Another thought I had to push away, for now.

"If Philippa is still up there, she would know. I'll go up and check."

"And if you could bring more blood, that would be great," I added as we went to the front door.

"Sure. I'll be right back." He turned and pressed his lips to my forehead before he went.

"What was that for?"

He shrugged. "I don't know why, but I feel the need to kiss you, or at least let you know I love you every time we're about to be away from each other."

That was sweet, but… "You're only going upstairs," I teased.

"And after everything we'd been through, you think that makes a difference?"

18

PHILIPPA

"Vance?" I breathed, jogging out to the living room. There he was, staring at me with wide, hopeful eyes I wished I could gouge out.

Stop thinking that way. He'll see right through you. This is Vance. You love Vance. You just got him back. You're thrilled he's returned.

"I'm so sorry," I whispered, throwing myself into his open arms. "I don't want to fight with you. We've lost so much time already." *Vance, I know you're in there, somewhere. I love you. We'll get you out.*

When I looked up into his eyes, I wished there was a way to get through to the real Vance, to let him know I knew what was happening. To assure him it would all be over soon.

I hoped it would, at any rate.

"I don't want to lose you again," he whispered, running his fingers over my cheek, stroking it with his thumb before cupping my chin and pulling me in for a kiss.

It was sheer force of will that got me through it without screaming as his mouth moved over mine. I was right. His kiss wasn't the same at all. How could I have been so determined to believe him?

Because I loved Vance and wanted the lies to be true.

I forced a laugh after the kiss ended, and we stood in each other's arms, foreheads touching. "You'll never lose me." I closed my eyes and allowed myself to pretend I was talking to the real, true Vance. "You know how we are. We fight, we snipe at each other, but we always find a way back to what matters."

"I love you."

My skin crawled, but I focused every bit of concentration I possessed on pretending. "I love you, too, Vance. I always have."

It was a relief to pull away, to end the moment. I wasn't sure how long I could pretend his touch didn't nauseate me. "And you know what else?"

"What?" He was still so tender, so gentle.

Vance had to know what was going on, didn't he? What was he going through? Anything like what I was suffering?

I forced a smile. "I was wrong to be so stubborn. There's nothing wrong with you knowing where the body is; it makes perfect sense. I'm sorry I started a fight. You don't deserve that."

If he sensed something was off, he didn't show it. "You're sure? I don't want you to feel like I'm pushing you."

It was almost enough to make me laugh, the whole charade. Did he feel the same way? I would've bet it was all beneath him, having to pretend this way, debasing himself when he was the most powerful and fearsome of the Ancients.

"I'm sure. I don't want anything standing between us now. Let's start off with a clean slate, and this is the perfect way to do that."

"All right. If you want to."

Was Vance looking through his own eyes, or had Valerius

pushed him back into some dark corner of his own mind? I searched those familiar eyes for some hint, some trace of him, and found nothing. How did I ever believe him? It was a sad example of what a person in love was willing to explain away if it meant having their loved one back.

I took him by the hand and led him out through the front door, to the elevator. Would Fane's plan be in place? I could only hope so. While I didn't want to rush things, I also couldn't stand the thought of being with Valerius for another minute. I wanted to scrub off my skin anywhere he'd touched me.

"Where are we going?" he asked as we stepped into the elevator car.

"You'll see."

"Is it far?"

"Not very." I glanced up at him. "Why would I want to be far away from the body, right? I've been guarding it with my life ever since that day."

I didn't need to explain which day I was referring to. We both knew all too well.

The corridor was dark, as usual, lit only with a few work lights.

"In the basement?" he murmured, looking back and forth. He was on edge, uneasy. Did he expect something? Sense something off?

"A little more secure than that," I assured him. "We're not rubes."

"Oh, I know, I know. You would never be sloppy with something this important."

I almost bit my tongue off, wanting to thank him for his faith in me and my family. He was the one being sloppy with his choice of words. If I didn't know who he really was, we might have had a fight over it right outside the vault.

"Here we are," I announced, coming to a stop next to the familiar door. It looked just like any of the other doors we'd passed, and with good reason. We could hardly have hung a sign announcing the room's true purpose.

"This?" he asked, raising an eyebrow.

"You'll see." *Oh, you'll see, all right*. I could hardly wait, even as my heart hammered out of control while the door swung open and led to the second door with its electronic keypad.

"A vault?" he asked, and I caught a hint of appreciation in his voice.

"Impressed?"

He chuckled. "A little."

If he thinks this is impressive...

I mentally crossed my fingers as I entered the code to unlock the vault. If there was no one but Valerius inside, we were all sunk. What would I do if that was the case? Lock us all in? What if he could escape through the walls or something? Create a portal? *Please, be in there, Fane*.

At first, all I saw was the same body, against the wall and wrapped in blankets, as I'd left it. My heart clenched in despair, until I noticed a shadowy figure in the corner, not ten feet from the body.

Valerius didn't notice. He was too busy hurrying inside, making a beeline for his body. It wasn't until I closed the door behind us, sealing the room off, that he turned with a look of confusion.

"What are you doing?" he hissed.

"Philippa, stay far away." Fane stepped out of the shadows, into the light of the single lantern which burned at the side of the body.

I knew well enough not to ask questions, pressing myself into the corner by the door. Scott was nearby—I had never been so glad to see him, and I reached for his hand. He clasped it, moving closer to me, shielding me—I supposed from what was to come.

"What is this?" Valerius glanced around through Vance's eyes, taking in the scene.

One by one, others stepped out of the darkness.

A beautiful woman in robes the color of red wine, with black hair that tumbled down her back, and large, all-seeing eyes.

A black-haired man who wore an expression I could only describe as haughty. He gave me a bad feeling.

The entire situation gave me a bad feeling, as Fane and the other two closed in on Valerius.

"What do you think you're doing?" he snarled. "Who do you think you're dealing with?"

"We know who we're dealing with, Valerius," Fane announced.

"You're wrong. I'm Vance."

"No. You aren't." My voice was shaky, but loud. "You're not Vance. I should've seen it from the beginning. I know he's in there, but you are, too."

"And it's time you returned to your own body and left the rest of us in peace." Fane made a move as if to take him by the arms, but Vance's body was younger and faster than his. Maybe even stronger.

He ducked Fane's lunge then moved toward Scott and me.

Fane glanced at Scott, who understood his silent command and sprang into action. He let go of me and threw his arms around Valerius's shoulders, knocking him off-balance just long enough for Fane to take hold of one of his arms. Scott took the other one.

"What do you think you're doing?" Valerius yelled in Vance's voice. I wanted to cover my ears and pretend I couldn't hear any of it, that it wasn't happening. When he looked so much like him and sounded like him, it wasn't easy to separate the two of them.

I didn't want to think of Vance hurting, but it needed to be done. He had to be freed.

"What has to be done," the dark-haired man replied in a deep, sonorous voice. He exchanged a glance with the woman, who nodded.

The two of them closed their eyes, both chanting in unison just under their breath.

I couldn't understand what they were saying, only that the energy in the closed-off room seemed to heighten. It made the hair on the back of my neck stand straight up.

"What? No. No!" Valerius fought against Fane and Scott, who grunted in the struggle to hold on to him.

A halo of light surrounded the two chanting figures, which then extended itself to wrap around Valerius's body and Vance's. He closed his eyes, his head snapping back.

"Don't hurt him!" I gasped, but the sound of my voice was lost in the chanting, grunting, and fighting. I reached for them but didn't leave the corner, afraid to move in case I got in the way or destroyed something.

The energy spiked, the force pressing me against the wall, ripping the air from my lungs. Valerius or Vance or whoever he was by now cried out once, in pain or anger, or both, before convulsing violently.

Fane and Scott exchanged a look of panic as the body in their arms shook as though it was being electrocuted before it went limp.

And then, everything stopped.

The glowing light seemed to evaporate, the chanting went silent.

I could breathe again. "Oh, no," I whimpered, my eyes

filling with tears as I went to Vance. "Is he breathing? Did he—"

"He should be fine in a little while," the woman said in a soothing voice. "He'll need to rest."

"Why won't he open his eyes?" I demanded, never looking away from him.

His head lolled onto his shoulder, eyes closed, mouth half-open.

"Are you certain it worked?" Fane asked, sounding as uncertain as I did.

"If I didn't know better," the dark-haired warlock or whoever he was replied, "I would think you were questioning my abilities."

I turned to him, ready to mouth off and likely get myself into trouble, when movement from the floor caught my eye.

For the first time since we'd brought him to the vault—no, since before then, since before he'd been imprisoned in that tomb of roots which had kept him in place for endless years.

Before I could call anyone's attention to him, Valerius's eyes opened.

19

SCOTT

Vance was dead weight in my arms, out like a light.
Philippa did everything but hang off him, wrapping her arms around his neck.

"He's already heavy enough," I grunted.

"Let's set him down over here," Fane suggested, and we half-dragged him to the wall before letting him slide to the floor.

Philippa sank to his side, holding him up, stroking his head as it rested on her shoulder.

"Vance, please, wake up," she blubbered. "Please, don't leave me again."

"He's definitely alive. He's breathing, see, his chest is moving." I touched her shoulder, but she didn't seem to notice. She was too wrapped up in him.

There were other things happening. Such as Valerius sitting there with his eyes open. But that was the only part of him that had moved up to this point. He might as well have been a wax figure.

Elazar and Branwen had done it. I had to give her credit

for whatever part she had taken in the spell. For someone as small as she was, there was a lot of power in her.

Was I praising a witch? Even to myself?

There was no time to explore this, as Valerius began to fully awaken.

I tensed, as did everyone else in the room, other than Vance, who groaned softly in Philippa's arms.

I glanced down to find her holding him tightly, staring daggers at the ancient one across the vault.

He blinked, looked around. Emitted a growl. "What have you done to me?"

"What needed to be done," Fane reminded him, taking two steps closer.

Valerius fought his way to his feet slowly, so slowly, and I found myself straining to hear if his old bones and joints creaked in protest. His skin was like paper, revealing every vein running under it.

I wasn't sure how he was still alive after what he'd just gone through. I had held on to Vance during all of it and had felt the way his body shook and convulsed as energy pulsed through it.

"How dare you?" he growled, glaring at each of us in turn. "How dare you think you have the right to infringe on my plans? Who do you think you are?"

"I believe you know who I am," Elazar reminded him, smirking as always.

"Oh, yes. I know all of you, and still, I ask how you can begin to believe you have any right to interfere with forces so far beyond you?"

"Spare us." Elazar sighed. "If you were so far beyond us, we wouldn't have been able to get you down here and pull you out of that young vampire's body. You aren't impressing any of us with your grand statements."

"And since you already had your revenge on Lucian," Fane added, "what purpose was there in possessing Vance any longer?"

A slow smile spread across his face, the faded eyes lighting up. "I had several further uses for his body." He looked at Philippa, his smile widening.

Fane almost got to Valerius before I could stop him.

"He's just trying to get under your skin," I muttered as I held him back. "Don't give him the satisfaction."

"Don't speak of my daughter that way. Don't you even mention her," Fane warned.

I half-expected his fangs to descend. Until I remembered he no longer had them.

"Enough of this," Valerius announced, the light extinguishing, the smile vanishing. "Where is Nivia? We've waited far too long already."

Uh-oh. I had forgotten about her. Fane stiffened; clearly, he had, too. We looked at Elazar. It seemed his news to tell.

I wondered if we should be here, if I should take Philippa and get out. Memories of what had happened on Shadowsbane flashed through my mind as my eyes darted back and forth between Elazar and Valerius.

"What should we do?" I whispered to Fane.

He shook his head only once. To silence me? To admit he didn't know what to do? I couldn't tell.

Elazar raised his chin, staring at the ancient one down the bridge of his nose. "She's dead."

I tensed, ready to defend myself and my sister if need be. It seemed the entire room held its breath as Valerius processed this.

"What did you say?" he murmured.

"I said, she's dead," Elazar shrugged. "At my hand. I killed her on Shadowsbane Island. Ask Fane and the boy." He pointed my way. "They were there."

Valerius didn't confirm this information with us. He never took his eyes from Elazar's smirking face.

He then raised his hands, intent on tearing into that face as he flew toward his enemy. An ear-splitting scream of rage filled the vault.

Elazar merely raised a hand, shooting a bolt of pure energy at Valerius. It was as though he hit an invisible wall, his body stopping suddenly before rebounding and hitting the floor.

I knew the feeling. Elazar had done the same to me back at the mausoleum.

Only I had lived through the experience.

Valerius had not.

His eyes were wide, unseeing, as he settled against the concrete. Then, in front of all of us, his body decomposed. It dried, crumbled, turned to dust surrounded by old robes.

The entire process couldn't have taken five seconds.

Philippa's long, low moan pulled my horrified attention out of the situation. "What… what did you just do? He's dead? Just like that?"

"What does it look like?" Elazar studied the dust that had only moments earlier been a living, breathing person. "Good riddance. He lived far too long and caused far, far too much pain."

"I don't believe this. After everything that's happened." Philippa stared up at me, searching for answers.

I was at a loss. "Trust me. Things happen that quickly sometimes. You don't even want to know what I've seen."

"What about the line? The bloodline? If we are all descended from Valerius, and when he dies his descendants will die…"

Branwen shook her head. "The line was broken."

"What?" I looked at Philippa and Fane. "Did you two know of this?"

Philippa shrugged. Of course. All she cared about was Vance.

So I looked to Fane again. "Well?"

"I wasn't aware." That's all Fane said.

I frowned, baffled.

Elazar glanced up at us after examining his handiwork. "Well. I believe my job here is done." And like that, he was gone. He disappeared.

I looked back at Philippa, who was more dumbfounded than ever.

"See what I mean?"

20

VANCE

Of all the surreal, unthinkable things that had gone on in my life to this point, the most surreal of any of them was opening my eyes and finding myself in control of my body again.

I blinked once, twice, flexing my fingers, moving my toes. They seemed to work, though it felt like I was moving through semi-set cement. Even that tiny movement was exhausting.

"Vance? Are you there? Are you with me?" I was in Philippa's arms, resting against her body, and that was good.

So very good. I could finally feel her instead of knowing it was Valerius who touched her, who kissed her.

"I'm here," I mumbled.

Even my mouth felt too heavy to move, my tongue like a thick slab in my mouth. My body was mine again, but not mine. If the exhaustion hadn't been so complete, I might have been angry. As it was, all I wanted was to sleep.

"Please, open your eyes and look at me. Please." She touched my chin, tilting my head back against her shoulder. She was so warm, soft but strong. She was always strong. And she had found a way around his lies. She had seen through him, the way I knew she would.

I had warned him.

During our walk, when he'd nearly put my fists through window after window of the shops we'd passed on the street. He'd finally resorted to balling my hands up and shoving them into my pants pockets. They had clenched tight enough to hurt.

You're pushing too hard. I knew you would, I had taunted him. *How does it feel to know you're not in control, the way you thought you were?*

He'd snarled loud enough to get the attention of a couple walking past. They had hurried on, heads lowered.

I'll kill her and make you watch, just like I killed that weak little witch in ShadesRealm. You thought that was bad, I know. You all but begged me to stop. It was your hands that did it. You felt her hot blood on them, didn't you? And you wanted to drink it, because that's all you are. A weak, pitiful vampire who can't control himself when there's blood in the air. I wonder what Philippa's blood will smell like? I wonder if you'll want to drink it?

Stop, stop, stop! Shut up! I'd wanted to warn him away from that, to make it known I was strong enough to fight back and overcome him if I tried. I'd settled for knowing I could do it if needed and left it there.

She's smarter than you give her credit for, I'd reminded him.

And I was right. It brought a smile to my face.

I opened my eyes, looking up into hers. There was something I needed to tell her while I had the chance, in case something else happened and I lost the chance again.

"I love you."

"Oh, Vance." She kissed my forehead, my cheeks. "I love you, too."

"I was there all the time, listening and watching. It drove

me crazy, knowing he was..."

"We don't have to talk about it now. Or ever, really. You just rest, okay? There's all the time in the world."

"I only want you to know... why I let it go on." I had to explain it. I couldn't let another minute go by without explaining it. "I wanted to fight him. I wanted to stop him. But I was afraid for you. That he would hurt you to get back at me."

"I understand." Her hand was tender as she ran it down the side of my face. "You don't have to explain yourself. Who knows what he was capable of?"

She had no idea. I did, and that was all the more reason for me to fear what he could do to hurt her. Or worse. Because I had felt Tabitha's blood on my hands. I had watched her die, had listened to her final rasping breaths.

A strange woman knelt at my side, touching my forehead, my throat, my wrists. "He needs to rest," she announced.

If I'd had the strength, I would've asked how long she'd trained to learn the skills it took for a diagnosis like that one. Anyone with eyes could see I needed to rest. I was falling apart.

"We'll take him up to the apartment." Philippa wasn't asking a question. "Scott, help him."

Scott slid an arm under my shoulders, picking me up until I was on my feet. Not a lot of good that did, as I couldn't support my weight. "Come on, buddy. Let's get you out of this place."

I looked over my shoulder at what was left of Valerius sitting in a pile on the floor. "What about him?" I asked no one in particular.

"What about him?" Fane echoed. "He'll stay there until somebody gets around to cleaning him up. If anyone ever does. I doubt I'll lose sleep over it."

Lose sleep over it. We didn't sleep. I wondered if that was just an expression or if there really was something different about him. I'd felt it, even when Valerius had possessed me. He wasn't the same as me or Philippa or Scott. Not anymore.

I was too tired to think about it, too wrung out. I let Scott help me out of the vault and back to the elevator.

Philippa watched closely the entire time, as though she was waiting for something. For what? For me to fall apart? For Valerius to come back through my eyes, my words? That wouldn't happen. He was dead. Finally, for good. I never thought I would be so grateful.

But I had watched my father being murdered. By my own hands.

I closed my eyes, hoping the images would fade. That didn't help. I didn't think it ever would.

"You'll feel better soon enough," the woman in the red robes murmured as she rode with us in the elevator. "Rest all you can. Feed, if possible."

"We have plenty of blood in the refrigerator and more in our bank downstairs," Philippa assured me. "You'll be fine."

"I have no doubt," I murmured, eyes still closed.

The bell sounded, signaling our arrival at the top floor. It would feel good to be in the penthouse and be able to control my body, my voice.

They helped me to the sofa, which I sank into with a sigh. Just that little bit of movement had wiped me out even further.

Philippa joined me, seemingly glued to my side. I wouldn't be able to shake her easily. Not that I wanted to.

"I'm so relieved for you," she murmured, curling up beside me. "I was so scared when it was all happening, and there was this light..."

"I remember that part." I chuckled. My voice sounded

far away.

"And you were shaking..."

"We don't need to go over this right now, do we?" I asked, turning my head slightly to look down at her. It took so much effort, but she needed to know how I felt about this. "I would rather not relive that right now. If you don't mind."

Her eyes went wide. "I'm sorry."

I sighed, remembering how Valerius had wormed his way into her head when they were arguing. He had taken all of the memories I had of her, had mined me for information and violated even the most cherished, personal moments. All for his own gain, all so he could twist her up and use her.

Here I was, so soon after she had been hurt, being sharp. "No. I'm sorry. You didn't deserve that. There's been so much going on. So very much. And I'm trying to make sense of it."

"I understand."

"You were always the one thing I was most concerned about. I want you to know that."

"Thank you." She closed her hand over mine.

Scott returned from the kitchen, carrying a bag of blood. "Here. Start building your strength up."

"Thanks." I drank deeply, savoring the taste even though it was synthetic. In my state of weakness, what I craved more than anything was real blood. I hadn't experienced a craving this strong in decades.

Once the bag was drained of its contents, Scott took it away. He seemed strangely subdued. We had never been close, but I'd spent enough time with all the Bourke siblings to know their personalities. I wasn't the only one who'd been through quite an experience, it appeared.

Fane and the witch had disappeared somewhere. Scott went down the hall, probably to his room. That left Philippa and me alone for the moment.

"I am so, so sorry," I whispered, resting my head against the pillows Philippa had stacked behind me. "I wanted so much to protect you, to be with you. To at least tell you it wasn't me you were with earlier."

She winced, clearly uncomfortable at the memory of those moments. "It's all right. I understand, really. I'm angry with myself, if anything."

"Why?"

"Because I knew something was off, but I didn't want to believe it. I didn't listen to my instincts. Shouldn't I know better? I'm not a child. I've been taking care of myself for a long time, and a lot of that depends on listening when my gut tells me something is wrong. I didn't listen. I blocked it out."

"You didn't want to listen."

"No. I didn't." She shook her head, looking as though she was ready to burst into tears. "I wanted it to be you. I wanted it badly enough to ignore everything that told me it wasn't you."

The pain she tried so hard to hide tore at me. I pulled her into my arms, wishing that was enough but knowing better. "If anything, it was better for you to play along. Who knows what he would've done if you had fought back or let him know you were wise to him?"

"I would've hurt him."

I chuckled. "Hey, remember. You wouldn't have been fighting the old man. You would've been fighting me. I'm pretty strong."

"Hmm. We would have to see, wouldn't we?" She pressed herself to me, practically crawling into my lap. "I don't ever want to let you go again. Not ever."

"I feel the same way. I couldn't let myself think about you while he was in my head. He would see, he would know. He already knew too much. He already did too many terrible things."

She raised her head, looking at me with tears in her eyes. "I'm so sorry about your father. I really am. It's terrible, what he did."

I nodded, taking a deep breath to hold back the wave of heartache her words brought. There would be time to think about that, time I hadn't been able to take up to that point because of Valerius's presence. He'd spent the entire duration of his possession searching for ways to take advantage of me. Leaving myself open to greater damage would've been foolish.

And it wasn't the thing I felt worst about.

"I know on some level my father would've met a bad end no matter who delivered the death blow," I reasoned, running a hand through her fiery hair as I spoke. It was so soft, smelled so sweet. She didn't know how soothing it was to touch this one small part of her. "I do wish it hadn't come at my hands, but I can rationalize it when I have to. It might be the only way to get through this—the ability to rationalize what happened."

"Whatever you need to do for yourself," she murmured as she tried to snuggle back in at my side.

I stopped her. "There's something else. Something I feel even worse about. I don't know if I'll ever be able to forget it, or if there's a way to make it up to those who will suffer the worst over it."

"Oh, Vance." Her face fell. "What happened? What did he make you do?"

I wondered if I should tell her at all. If I would only come to regret it later. "There have been enough secrets and lies and half-truths between us. Wouldn't you agree? I mean, isn't that a large part of the reason why we fell apart?"

"A large part, yes," she agreed, nodding slowly.

"However..." I closed my eyes, struggling to put words to my thoughts. "However, I'm so afraid that you won't be able to forgive me when you hear about this. I don't want you to always see this when you look at me, to imagine what I did."

"Whatever it was, you didn't do it. I can't say it enough."

"You're right. You can't say it enough. It'll never be enough."

She glanced down at her hands, picking at her nails the way she always used to when something uncomfortable was going on. "I want to say that you don't have to tell me, but I'm afraid I'll always want to know."

"That's what I mean. I don't want it to come between us. Even if it doesn't right away, it will in the future."

"So, it really is that serious?"

"Not just serious. More like... severe."

"Oh, no." She breathed deeply, letting it out slowly before deciding. "Out with it, then. I would rather hear it. And you know I won't judge you or blame you. It might be difficult for me to hear, and I have to admit, you're frightening me more than a little. You didn't wipe out an entire neighborhood or a bunch of kids, did you—he?" she corrected at the last moment.

It was too late. She had already slipped. I let it go.

"No, nothing on such a large scale. It was a woman. She was alone. In a tower."

She closed her eyes. The sudden color in her cheeks and nose told me she was trying not to cry. "All right."

"I was in there—we were, I should say, him and me. Locked in a cage. I'm still not sure why, the person who did it never explained. He was a shade. I felt as though I had seen him before. I think he may have been at the meeting where I... Where Valerius..."

"I know what you're saying."

I cleared my throat to get rid of the brick of a lump lodged in it. "He never explained why he put me—us—in the cage. But it was silver, so there was no getting out. We were there for hours. I was sure we'd be there forever, that it was some sort of massive cosmic joke. The shade had freed us from the dungeon, only to leave us in a cage in a tower. I mean, why do something like that?"

I remembered so clearly the confusion, the certainty that we'd never get out. That Valerius would never leave me, and we would never leave that tower. The worst was the not knowing why.

"Valerius raged, roared, demanded we find a way to get out. But what way was there? See, he never thought about my limitations when he took my body. He could handle silver, but I couldn't. Which meant he couldn't—not that it stopped him from trying." I held up my hand, where a mostly-healed burn still scarred on my palm.

Philippa picked it up and kissed it. "I'm sorry."

"He soon found out there was no getting out. Until... until she got there. The woman. It was her room, her tower. She didn't expect us, that was for sure."

"Who was she?"

"Valerius pleaded with her," I continued, unwilling to answer until I got the entire story out. "He begged her to be let out, told her he had no idea why he was there. That he'd been locked up while under someone's spell, that he couldn't fight back, that he was afraid and hurt. He used this burn to convince her and told her how hungry he was."

"Oh, no..."

"She was a good soul," I murmured, remembering how concerned she had seemed. "And I felt as though I knew her, too, though she didn't appear to remember me. I was a small part of her former life. I know that, now. She was different from the way I remembered her. Part shade. I know that now, too. I had time to think about it. it was safer than thinking about you."

"What happened once she freed you?"

"He went on the attack, of course. He couldn't leave it alone. It wasn't enough she'd let us go. He had to kill her. She went on the defensive, bared her fangs. It was strange, seeing a shade with fangs. She was strong, too. Just not strong enough. Not as strong as me."

She squeezed my hand.

My voice broke, but I managed to continue. "I was too weak to fight him. I tried. I did. I saw what was coming, and she didn't deserve it. I wanted to save her. There was no way. And in my head, all the time, he laughed. He delighted in it. He savored throwing her to the floor, her groan of pain, the way she tried to scramble from us. He reached for her and held her down, hand around her throat. And… my fangs…"

She covered her face with her hands, and I stopped. There was hardly a reason to continue. I didn't need to tell her about tasting the blood, about begging Valerius to pull away before I had to drink it. Only his disgust at the idea of drinking a shade's blood stopped him from feasting on her.

"He did the strangest thing," I remembered. "He went away, stepped back, let me take over. Maybe he wanted to sit back and laugh as I fumbled through trying to make her last moments a little less lonely. I told her how sorry I was, that it wasn't me, that someone had control over me. I don't know if she believed me or not. I hope she did."

"Did she say anything?"

"Oh, yes. She told me to tell her daughters and her son how much she loved them. Anissa, Sara, Allonic."

Philippa let out a cry of dismay.

As I'd known she would.

21

PHILIPPA

"You're sure? Those three names?" I knew he was sure.

He didn't need to respond.

I covered my face with my hands, shaking my head. It all came together. Allonic was the shade who'd locked Vance in the tower. Why, I didn't know. He had his reasons for everything he did. Did he know she was dead?

Did he know she wouldn't be if he hadn't stolen Vance from the dungeon?

My heart broke for him. For Vance. Even for the girls. I didn't like them, but that didn't mean it made me happy to know their mother had been murdered. My mother had been murdered, too.

"You're close with them?" Vance's voice was flat.

I shook my head. "That's not the right word. But I know them. Anissa is Jonah's... woman. Consort. I don't know what to call her. But we're not close."

"Even so."

"Even so." Fate was too cruel sometimes. Why did it have to be Allonic who brought them together? Why did it have to be Vance who he caged in that tower? He couldn't have known, of course, but he had to know by now what had happened.

Had Allonic found her? A fresh wave of grief hit me. He had taken a big chance for my sake. He had been captured because of it, too. Tortured. And he had likely found his mother's body in that tower, knowing when he saw the empty cage it had been Valerius who killed her.

Vance glanced away, suddenly very interested in something off in the distance. "I thought it would be best for you to know this, even if you can't look at me the same way again."

"No. Don't say that." I reached for him, but he flinched away, and my heart sank even further.

"Come on, Philippa. You're going to sit there, sad like that, then tell me you could ever forgive what I did?"

"You didn't do it! And I'm sad for Allonic, but I'm sad for you, too. Not because nothing will ever be the same between us. I'm not worried about us right now. I'm worried about you. My heart hurts for you. I wish I could take this away from you."

I took his face in my hands.

He tried to pull away, but I was having none of it.

"Look at me. Believe me. I don't hold this against you. You couldn't stop him. I can't imagine what that must've been like for you. But I do not blame you. I never will."

"How can you ever look at me the same way again, after hearing this?"

"Because I know you." My hands dropped from his face, landing on his chest. "I know who you are. We've had our problems, yes. You've hurt me in the past. You've done some things that made me want to forget you ever existed. You were responsible for that, but it's all over now. This?

What you told me just now? That's not you. You didn't do it."

"I don't see how you can forgive it."

"Because you don't see how you can forgive yourself. But you have to try. You can't live this way. We can't."

He blinked. "We?"

My hands landed in my lap, and I blushed. "I might be going too far. But if there's a future for us... If that's what you want..."

"When did you mature so much?" he asked, the slightest smile touching his lips.

I smiled, too. It was good to hear him lighten up, even just a little. "I've been through a few things, too. It's been a pretty busy time for so many of us."

"We'll have to catch up on all of it."

"We will. For now, you'll have to rest up." I kissed him—there he was, there was his kiss—right before Fane walked in.

He sized us up with a quick glance and offered a gruff smile.

"I'm glad to see you're doing better." He nodded at Vance.

"Thanks to you. I don't know how much longer I could've been under the control of that monster before I lost my sanity."

"I shudder to think." He looked at me. "And you."

"Me?" I stood and went to him.

"I wanted to say goodbye before leaving."

"You're leaving again? So soon?"

He frowned, his eyes sad, then nodded. "Yes. I have to. I don't want to. You have no idea how much I would like to stop going from place to place. There are times, like now, I wish I could settle down again and..."

I could only try to accept and understand what his life had become. It wasn't easy. I certainly didn't want to. The whole business of living in between—he was my father, but he wasn't anymore—was worse than tiresome. It was exhausting, depleting.

But it was our life.

"I understand." Even so, I threw my arms around him before he could react. "Thank you. I know it couldn't have been easy to find the people you needed."

He stiffened, which I had expected, but replied, "I wanted to at least know you were happy. That much, I could do."

A single tear rolled down my cheek.

I wanted to ask about the change in him, why he seemed so different from the way he used to be, but it didn't seem like the right time. The right time might never come. Another thing I had to accept. I had Vance back, and he was a gift from my father, and that would have to be enough.

None of us expected the front door to open when it did—and Jonah was not who I expected to see striding into the penthouse.

Judging by the shock on his face as his gaze swept over the room, he hadn't expected to see us, either.

22

ALLONIC

Two of Garan's so-called foot soldiers waited outside the throne room, one on either side of the arched doorway carved into the stone.

Throne room. The leader of the shades didn't belong on a throne. He belonged among all of us, working alongside us to maintain the safety of what we considered sacred. To help us fulfill our destiny as the keepers of memory and knowledge.

He'd never cared for that, any more than his father had.

My father had cared, and he would've been the greatest of all leaders. If only he'd had the chance.

Garan barely glanced my way as I pushed past his soldiers. He waved a hand to call them off when they made a move toward me. He was pacing back and forth in front of the throne, at the base of the stairs leading up to it.

"Leave us. I'm certain my half-breed cousin has plenty to say about many things, judging by his insistence."

Only when we were alone did I speak. "Have I heard correctly? Did you take a prisoner who trespassed in my mother's tower?"

"Your mother's tower," he sneered, then shook his head.

"You did always have difficulty with the simple things, didn't you? Your mother did not own that tower. She owned nothing. Everything she had, she had thanks to the benevolence of my father. It was as his brother would've wanted, or so he always said."

"Regardless," I growled, barely holding my temper at bay, "I've heard about the trespasser in the tower. It's true, I assume."

"It's true."

"And you believe this is an act of war?"

"I do," he sneered. "What else? Everyone knows we draw a hard line when it comes to trespassing on our land. It's no secret. And considering I only just met with the two of them and even provided an escort through ShadesRealm, so they could examine the tower themselves..." He shook his head.

I frowned, lost again. "What do you mean? Who had an escort?"

"Gregor and that... associate of his. Whoever she is to him. They both knew better, but she came back. Alone. Without permission. That, I cannot abide."

His associate. My head spun. The room shifted around me. It couldn't be. White-haired. I had assumed that meant Anissa.

Felicity had white hair, too.

"What is it?" he asked, eyeing me closely. "Do you know her?"

"Vaguely," I lied, waving a hand as my stomach turned in pure agony. "She's a friend of my half-sister's."

"Right. I often forget you're indirectly related to that lot."

A lie, and we both knew it. He was keenly aware of my heritage, of the fact my mother once consorted with the king of the fae.

Felicity. Sweet Felicity.

I had willed myself to forget about her, told myself time and again she'd never forgive me for what had led to Tabitha's death.

She had come back. For what purpose? If she'd found what I'd found back at the tower—with the exception of the cage, which I had removed from the room—she knew Tabitha was dead. She had to know. Why would she return?

Unless...

She was looking for me.

Would the torment ever end? Would the ripples which extended out from my one act of greed ever cease expanding?

I fought to speak over the lump in my throat. "So. It's clear my mother is dead. Everyone knows it."

"We do," he replied, arching his brow. "Is there anything you would like to say about that?"

"What could I possibly have to say about it?"

"I don't know." He shrugged. "Perhaps you could illuminate me on how your peaceful, tranquil mother met such a grisly end? I did not see the body, I admit, but I saw the aftermath."

I ground my teeth.

He chuckled grimly. "You could at least have cleaned up the room."

My head snapped up, eyes meeting his. My fangs threatened to descend, the vampire nature I'd inherited from my mother surging in my veins. An attack would be the worst mistake I could make—which he was aware of, which was why he'd goaded me into the rage surging through me.

I took a deep breath, easing myself back into clear thinking. I needed to keep my wits about me if there was any hope of freeing Felicity and preventing a terrible war.

"I was a bit more concerned with removing my mother's

body from the tower," I replied, my face as blank as I could make it.

He nodded. "And after that? Where have you been?"

"Taking care of things which needed to be taken care of."

"Do you know who killed her?" he asked.

We silently appraised each other. I placed myself in his position. Why would he know, unless Valerius had gone on a rampage through ShadesRealm? I doubted the Ancient would be so foolish. He must have slipped out somehow. Who knew what an Ancient was capable of. Possibly even portals. For sure, one that old would know some of the ways in and out of ShadesRealm.

If anyone else had discovered him, he would've killed them as well. Anything to make certain there was no way to trace him.

There was no reason to believe Garan was aware of who'd murdered Tabitha.

"No," I replied, my expression unchanging. I held his gaze, daring him to challenge the truth of my reply.

He didn't. "I would very much like to know who would dare perpetrate such a crime in ShadesRealm." Nothing of the fact an innocent woman had been murdered. He cared nothing for that.

"I'm sure you would. In light of this and the emotions the crime clearly inspired, it's natural anyone who cared for her would want to do anything possible to ease their pain. Isn't it?"

"You mean the trespassing fae," he surmised.

"Yes. Who else?"

"Again, the fae had their chance. They knew how I felt about their being here. I was generous in offering them passage when they requested it." He threw his arms up, every inch the put-upon leader. "How far is my generosity expected to reach? Don't you see how easy it would be for this generosity to be construed as weakness? I must use this situation as an opportunity to display my strength. Ressenden is dead, but I'm just as strong as unflinching as he. More so, even."

My hopes faded with every word from his mouth. He had no intention of being reasonable. This was a matter of pride.

More than that. "Besides. I've always felt a great affinity for Avellane. I traveled there once, you know, many years ago. Its beauty is unsurpassed. The fae do not deserve all of that beauty for themselves. It's selfish of them to hoard their treasures as they do—the gems and jewels so freely mined there."

His description brought to mind the dome of the Hermitage, which indeed was awe-inspiring. He cared nothing for its beauty, or the for the beauty of the land on which it sat. He wanted the jewels. He wanted the riches for himself.

"What's the point of starting a war over this?" I asked, grasping at straws in an attempt to change his heart. "Why not put together a trade agreement with the fae, instead? Gregor is reasonable. He wouldn't refuse you."

"What do I have to offer in return?" Garan scoffed.

"Easy. Your captive."

That wiped the smirk from his face. He even appeared to consider this—before shaking his head. "No. That won't work. The agreement would eventually have to come to an end, and I would no longer have leverage."

Rage threatened to tear through me. She was down there, in the dungeon, probably frightened and cold and alone, thinking I had deserted her. Seeing no end in sight. And I couldn't even manage to bargain for her. "You might be surprised what Gregor is willing to agree to if it means her safety," I argued.

"She means that much to him?"

I shrugged, unwilling to give up too much.

He frowned, but not for long. "I don't see why I should have to explain my reasoning to a half-breed, regardless of the fact we share blood. I never consented to your presence here. Get out. Stop wasting my time when I have so much to attend to."

He turned his back to me, ascending the stairs to his throne. There was nothing more for me to do at that point than to leave and think of another way to help her. I had to. There was no way I'd live with myself if someone else I cared for suffered because of me.

And I cared for her, more deeply than I'd ever cared for anyone else. I hoped she knew it.

"One more thing." Garan's voice carried across the cavernous room, pulling at me.

I turned to find him glaring down at me, hands at his hips, feet spread. The ruler, if only in his own mind.

"What is it?" I asked, careful to keep the disdain from my voice.

"Don't think about trying to free her."

I blinked, swayed by his insight but unwilling to reveal this. "Why would I?"

"I don't know—then again, I don't know or understand many things about you, shared blood or no shared blood. Every entrance leading into or out of these caves has an enchantment placed on it. No one without shade blood in their veins will be able to come or go. I thought you should be aware of that, in case you had any ideas."

I remained silent, merely turning with a sweep of my robes and striding from the throne room with my head held high.

Even as every last ounce of hope drained away.

23

CARI

It took another few days for me to decide the worst part about being a vampire was the lack of sleep. No sleep meant no dreaming. No escaping reality.

I couldn't dream about Gage. Even that slight bit of mercy was denied me as I struggled to get through life without him.

"How long do you think they'll keep him alive before they decide to kill him?" I asked Micah at one point, on the way back from a hunt.

We couldn't be as bold as we had at one time, when I first arrived in Paris. I felt uncomfortable with the idea of revisiting our old hunting grounds. That was where Gage had been captured, after all. What were the odds the league wouldn't keep returning to the same place to look for me, too?

After I had protested long enough and loudly enough for Micah to understand how serious I was, he had relented and announced we could start picking our victims from the parks nearby. He wasn't happy about that. I guessed the new arrangement didn't have the same sexy, dangerous feel.

But he wouldn't allow me to hunt alone. He insisted on being with me, no matter how many times I'd reminded him he could easily resume his activities in the streets surrounding the Moulin Rouge.

He sighed, sounding more than a little put out at yet another question about Gage. Could it be he was getting tired of talking about him, of answering the questions I asked? On the one hand, I understood how he'd feel that way. I also understood he might feel somewhat guilty for having allowed Gage's capture—indirectly, of course.

But we had fled to Paris for our safety, and Micah had assured us of that safety. I feared, on hearing his exasperated sigh, guilt nagged him the way it constantly tugged at my heart.

On the other hand, his irritation annoyed me. He had no right to act as though it was inconvenient, listening to my concerns. He was the one who never left me alone. I didn't ask for him to trail me, to insist on accompanying me on the hunt. I was more than capable of handling myself and had no intention of revealing myself to the rest of the world.

He didn't want to hear that.

"I honestly don't know," he muttered. "They might keep him alive indefinitely while waiting to find you. They might have killed him already."

"Oh." I leaned against the tunnel wall, still a distance from where it widened and became the makeshift headquarters of his clan. There were no bodies there, at least, no skulls marking the lives of untold thousands of Parisians who'd breathed and loved and died long before I was born. I didn't have to feel quite as creeped out there as I did once we moved deeper into the catacombs.

He took notice of my reaction and immediately doubled back to where I lingered. "I'm sorry. That was unforgivably insensitive of me. I forget myself sometimes. Please, forgive me."

"You're forgiven," I whispered, fighting against a wave of despair. Gage might already be dead. And, so long as I was being honest with myself, that might be preferable to the alternative of endless torture.

"Come. We just had a good hunt. Let's go home." Micah held his hands out to me, taking mine and leading me farther down the tunnel.

Home. Was it home? I lived in a graveyard, surrounded by the evidence of death. I caused death so that I might live. Was this what the rest of eternity would be like for me?

Gage once told me those of his clan, and indeed all the civilized clans, drank synthetic blood. No one had to die for them to survive.

"Have you ever thought of drinking processed blood?" I asked Micah as we continued on, the overhead bulbs lighting our way.

"What?" He laughed, as though this were the most absurd thing he'd ever heard. "Why would I choose to drink skimmed milk when I can feast on the richest, sweetest cream?"

"I was just wondering." More and more, it seemed as though we spoke a different language. He was so different from Gage, I wondered how they'd ever become friends in the first place.

"Is conscience getting in your way?" he asked.

"A little, I guess."

Gage understood. I didn't want to say it out loud and drive the point further home, but that didn't mean it wasn't true. He had always understood without being told that I still went through bouts of guilt and horror at what I was capable of. I wasn't certain those feelings would ever go away.

"Think of it like this, *cheri*," he advised as we reached the hub of the clan's home, with the tunnels then spreading out in different directions. "Without a hunt for a vampire to go on, what's the point of living? Without the hunt, without the chase and the conquering of another creature, there is nothing more to do. Wait to die, I suppose. Make love." A sly smile spread across his face.

But for Gage, there had been more to life. He'd had a family, a clan, friends. They had gone out on the town, all of them, had enjoyed themselves as best they could. Before I came along and ruined it all for him, of course.

I didn't give voice to any of this. I merely shrugged. "You have a point." I wouldn't entertain his allusions to lovemaking. I wouldn't give him the satisfaction.

He patted my hand before raising it to his lips. "I must bathe after all that exertion. I'll see you later."

"You know where to find me." I tried to sound cheerful—he deserved that much for protecting me the way he did—but it fell flat.

He had the grace to overlook this, walking away in the direction of his room before I turned to go to mine.

It was time to admit the truth I had been fighting for weeks, even before Gage's kidnapping.

I couldn't go on like this.

There was nothing real, nothing worthwhile. Killing for the sake of survival, and that was all. The rest of the clan all but ignored me—all but Naomi, that was. At least I still had her.

Micah was another story. I couldn't quite figure him out. I didn't feel as though I could trust him, which was the most disconcerting thing of all. I never knew quite how to take him. He seemed to be joking so much of the time, but there was an inevitable edge to every joke.

Not only that, but his advances had become more than I could fend off.

He was attractive. More than attractive. But he wasn't who I wanted—and not because no one would ever compare to Gage. He didn't care about anything or anyone, not really. I couldn't be with anyone who had no kindness in their heart.

It didn't matter the danger I'd be in if I left. I needed to do it. Every minute I spent here put them one minute closer to being discovered. If the league found me, and them by default, they'd all face my fate. I couldn't have that.

It was nearly dawn when we'd returned from the hunt, which meant I'd have to wait until sunset. Once that came, I'd leave. Even though I had no idea where I was going.

***

THE TUNNEL WAS EMPTY, WITHOUT THE NORMAL CHATTER floating along its length. Everyone had gone out to hunt.

I'd begged off, encouraging the others to go about their normal business without me. They didn't need to protect me for once. They could be free for the night. The way several pairs of eyes had lit upon hearing this wasn't lost on me. I weighed them down.

They wouldn't have to worry about that for much longer. I was doing the right thing, for sure.

I chose only what I absolutely needed to take with me —including one of Gage's shirts, one which reminded me the most of him—and shoved it into a backpack before slinging the pack over one shoulder and heading out of my room.

The silence all around me had an eerie feel to it, considering the number of skulls I passed as I tiptoed along the length of the tunnel. They watched, silent as always, witnessing what I was endeavoring to do. If they held an opinion, they didn't share. Just as well.

I reached the hub, with its spokes, and took the tunnel leading to the entrance. I could only hope none of them would come back early and run into me. If Micah found out…

What would he do? A flash of rebelliousness went off in my head. What could he possibly do to me? I wasn't a child. He didn't control me.

Right?

I made it down the tunnel and up the stairs to the overgrown, long-abandoned restrooms without being spotted.

The night was crisp, chill, and I took deep gulps of air once I reached the weed-choked courtyard behind the iron fence. All I'd have to do would be to go through the hole in the fence and out to the street, and I would be free.

Free for what? To destroy myself? I still didn't know exactly where I was going, but I had money left from what Gage and I had brought with us. I could get a hotel room, even if it was a crummy little hole-in-the-wall. I didn't need much. Just privacy. No questions.

"Decided to go hunting after all?"

Naomi's voice startled me to the point where I dropped my bag.

"Oh, God, you almost scared me to death." I laughed, one hand over my chest.

Damn it! What would she say? Would she tell the others?

"What are you doing out here?" she whispered, emerging from the shadows.

"Were you waiting here for me?" I took a backward step to put space between us. I didn't like the look in her eyes. They had never gleamed as they did now—at least, not when she was looking at me.

"Yes," she admitted simply, shrugging. "I knew you had a plan. You were a bit too eager to be left alone."

"You knew I was going to sneak out?"

"I did."

"You didn't try to stop me. You didn't tell anyone else."

"I did not."

"Why?"

"Because nobody needs to know. Especially not our mutual friend, who shall remain nameless at this time."

Why was she being so strange? Her voice was strained, as though she was in pain and struggled through it.

"What's wrong, Naomi? You seem..."

"Unwell?" she asked with a scornful laugh. "Perhaps I am. It's just that I've been fighting myself for days. There's something I absolutely must do, but I don't want to. Have you ever battled something like this? Knowing there's a course of action you need to take but being unwilling or unhappy over it?"

"Of course," I replied as my mind fought through what she was saying.

What did it mean to me? Was she going to hurt me? I was still young and strong enough I thought I'd be able to overpower her if it came down to that, though I didn't want to fight her or anyone.

"What did you do?" she asked.

"I decided to leave anyway."

Her laugh—warm, genuine, a laugh I had heard so many times—rang out through the night air, surprising me enough that I laughed, too.

"I do like you, Cari. I like you very much. Which is why I have to do what's causing me so much pain."

I braced myself, my senses on alert, the nerves jumping under my skin. What was she about to do? "You're in pain?

Why?" I asked, stalling, hoping she didn't have any tricks up her sleeve.

"Because I don't want to betray him. I've… I've loved him for so long." She raised her head slightly, the moonlight dancing off her face and illuminating tear-filled eyes. "I know I shouldn't. I know he probably doesn't even deserve it. He's never been very good to me, after all. He's never treated me as though I were any more than a diversion."

I struggled to keep up, knowing who she meant but unable to work out how she could possibly be betraying him now. Unless she planned on helping me escape while knowing how it would upset him. Could that be it?

She went on. "He has many good qualities. He's smart, he's a leader. He's generous to a point. I'm certain when he was human, before he was so badly hurt, he was a good man. Your Gage is a good man. They were friends. It makes sense, doesn't it?"

"It does." I had wondered about that very thing, hadn't I? But what was she getting at?

Her shoulders slumped as she shook her head. "I'm kidding myself. I search and search for good things about him. Some shred of decency, some humanity. That's all gone now. A century and more have wiped it away."

"What has he done?" I dared ask, afraid of the answer. "How could you possibly betray him right now?"

Her full mouth curved into a slow, sad smile. "You're such a sweet, precious girl. I wish we could be friends, real friends. Perhaps this is the first step in building a friendship I know I would've cherished if given a chance. You truly don't know what he's done? You don't have even the slightest inkling of suspicion?"

I was at a loss. She was swimming fast, her strokes sure

and strong, while I splashed around in a doggie paddle. Going nowhere.

"No. What am I missing?"

Something rustled in the leaves.

"Not here. Come with me," she whispered, taking me by the hand before I could protest and dragging me back to the door leading to the stairs, nearly running down the tunnel and not slowing until we reached my room.

"This isn't where I need to be right now," I protested when she finally let go of me.

"It is. For now, it is." She looked back and forth down the tunnel before stepping inside and closing the curtain behind us. We stood in the far corner, Naomi with her finger to her lips as she strained to hear any sound coming from the catacombs.

"We're alone," I mouthed.

She nodded. "All right. What I have to tell you, I have to tell quickly. There's a chance any of them could come back at any time. We don't want to be overheard."

"What is it, it already?" I was about ready to scream, she was being so cryptic.

"It's been over fifty years," she whispered, her eyes boring into mine, my hands in hers. "His name was Xavier, and I loved him. He was my mate. We had been with the clan for the better part of a decade by then. One night, he disappeared."

My eyes widened. "When? How?"

"I never knew exactly how. I only know he went out to hunt without me one night and never came back. The details were never revealed to me."

My heart ached for her. "I'm so sorry. I had no idea."

She nodded, the rest of the story coming out in a rush.

"Micah. He tried to comfort me, tried to make it better. But I grew suspicious of him. It seemed a bit soon to be, for lack of a better expression, putting the moves on me. That's how we described it back then. Insensitive of him, I thought at first, but then I began to wonder if he had anything to do with Xavier's disappearance. I told myself I was merely creating stories to soothe myself. But his description of what happened that night—he was with Xavier, you see—started to change, depending on when he was telling it. He saw a car drive away with my Xavier inside. Then, it was a group of men without a car who carried him off. Then, he simply vanished."

A chill crept into my bones, freezing me from the inside out. A car. While Micah was nearby.

"Finally, I began following him when he went out alone. I wanted to know where he went on the nights he wasn't hunting. There's an old prison, unused since the early nineteenth century, miles outside the city. He would disappear inside then come out alone. After three such instances, I waited for him to leave before going in to see what he was doing there."

"What was inside?" I breathed, completely captivated and horrified all at once. Afraid to hear the rest but aware I would die if I didn't.

"My Xavier. What used to be Xavier, at any rate. He'd starved for months by then, my poor beloved." Tears, pink-tinged, ran freely down her cheeks. "In a cell. He was nearly unrecognizable except for the clothing. And his eyes. The eyes were his. Oh, my love." She hung her head.

"What had happened to him?"

"He'd bitten off his own tongue," she wept. I gasped. "He was starving, starving, going mad with it. Starvation doesn't kill a vampire. It merely turns them into something beyond any imagining. It destroys the mind as well as the body. It's the worst torture imaginable."

"Was he still alive?"

She shook her head. "I never knew if he died because of what he'd done to himself, or because..."

"Of Micah," I breathed, sick with certainty.

"He wanted me. You see? He put my poor Xavier in that cell because he wanted me. Or because they'd fought, because of some perceived slight. I've never known for certain. I only know Micah knew he was there and visited more than once and did nothing to get him out. It stands to reason, then, that he was the one who put him there."

"You think..." I fell back against the wall, still holding her hands but unable to support my weight any longer. "You think that's what he did to Gage?"

"He wants you, *ma cherie*. He's mad for you. He would do anything. And..."

"And?"

"And I don't believe he ever quite forgave Gage for letting Georgina die. I know that story. I've spent many hours in his bed—oh, the times I've chastised myself for what I've become to him. What I allowed myself to become in spite of what I always knew he was capable of."

"Why did you? How could you, knowing as you did?"

She raised her eyebrows, shaking her head with an expression of baffled regret. "I knew I needed him. That's the hold he has on all of us. None of us believes we can make it in this world without the others. You know how there are men who lead cults? Who convince people of certain things which the rest of the world knows are patently false?"

"Sure."

"That's the case here, I believe. I did fall in love with him —or something like it. Nothing like what I had before, but a shadow of it. Even knowing what I've always known, but never had the courage to ask. Or perhaps I've never been crazy enough to ask. It doesn't strain credulity to imagine how enraged he could become. What he might do to me."

"Oh, Naomi. I'm so sorry." I couldn't imagine.

"I did ask him about it," she whispered. "Or, rather, I hinted. He refused to take the bait. But he was unsettled. Greatly so. I came a little too close to the truth for his comfort."

My entire body tingled. Gage. Was he going through the same torture Naomi had described?

"What can I do? I have to find him. I can't let this go on."

"And you won't. We won't. But there's one thing you must remember, absolutely and completely. You cannot forget this even for a minute."

"What is it?"

She squeezed my hands until they ached. "You cannot let him know you know. Under any circumstances. Or he might kill Gage just to cover his tracks."

24

GAGE

At first, I was certain the footsteps were only in my head. Yet another sick hallucination. I didn't know what was real anymore—except my thirst.

That was real. It was everything.

I bit back a groan as I raised my head to look through the iron bars. I couldn't move without groaning, moaning, crying out. Or just crying. The tears no longer came. My eyes were too dry.

The *snap-snap-snap* of shoes on the bare floor grew louder. I couldn't be imagining the sounds. They were too sharp and clear. But I had already seen so many things, heard so many things that could only have been in my head.

Terrible things.

"My old friend."

Micah again.

I had seen him many times. He had never spoken, though, choosing instead to stand outside the bars and stare with cold contempt. This was new.

I forced my eyes open, fixing them on him. It took a moment to bring him into focus, but I wasn't surprised once I did. He appeared much the same as always: handsome, sleek, well-groomed.

"You've looked better," he observed with a wry smile, as though he was reading my thoughts about him. "I suspect you've felt better, too."

"Is…? Are…?" My throat was so dry, it felt as though it bled when I tried to speak.

"Don't tire yourself," he urged. "I'm really here, if that's what you want to know. This is real. Not some horrible hallucination brought on by starvation."

I didn't have the strength to laugh. "How would you know?" I croaked.

"That starvation brings on hallucinations?" He laughed then, as though this was truly amusing. "You think you're the first person I've introduced to this old place? I'm no amateur, my friend. I know very well the stages of starvation and what a vampire is willing to do to stave them off. Have you yet made the acquaintance of the many plump rats who call this prison home?"

I grimaced. He merely laughed again.

"I thought not, in all honesty. You have too much pride. You're too… good to sink to that level."

There was only one thing I wanted to hear from him. "Cari?"

His eyebrows arched. "What about her? Come on. You can do it. Just tell me what it is you want to know, and I'll tell you." His chuckle was cold, nasty. "All right. I won't torment you. She's fine. Wonderful, in fact. Beautiful as ever, as strong a huntress as ever. Magnificent."

Good. At least she was safe and well. I could take a shred of solace in that.

"Don't you want to know if she misses you? If she worries about you?"

I shook my head, leaning it back against the wall. It hurt like hell, but I managed to conquer the worst of my reaction. I didn't yell or moan like a pitiful animal. That could come when he was long gone.

His handsome face crumpled in a frown of displeasure. "Why not? I would want to know. It would rip me to shreds, wondering if my love ever thought about me."

He didn't understand, and there was no way I could explain. I didn't need to ask because I knew. She would miss me. She would fear for me. It was her nature. He couldn't change that about her no matter how he tried.

Instead of replying to this, I whispered, "I'm sorry."

That stunned him. "Sorry? For what?"

My limited strength was already all but spent. I summoned all I had in order to stay conscious and lucid. "Georgina."

He shuddered visibly then raised his chin. "Why?" he challenged.

"You were right. I... could have done more. I could have... fought for you, as... you would have for me. I could have fought for her. I didn't. Not as a friend should."

His eyes narrowed, and he didn't speak for a long time. Just as well, since I needed to rest after expending so much energy. I didn't know where it was coming from—perhaps some deity had taken pity on me and would allow me this much, if nothing more.

"Where is this newfound understanding coming from?" he finally asked.

The life was gone from his voice. He was no longer taunting, teasing, enjoying himself.

"I understand now, because I love her. I had never loved before."

"Ah. I see." He nodded slowly, eyes narrowing further.

"You've been in my shoes, so to speak, and you know what it is to love another enough to break the most serious of laws. Laws of both men and vampires. Is that right?"

I nodded.

"Good." He smiled. "You'll have plenty of time to think this over. All the pain your weakness, your laziness, your inability to put yourself in another's place caused. You can think about it while Cari warms my bed."

My mouth fell open in surprise. I'd underestimated the depth of his hatred and cruelty—not that I had expected him to release me after what I'd said, but I hadn't expected him to grow even colder.

He was chuckling as he turned away, his footsteps echoing as he left me.

"You'll have roughly as long to think it over as I've been missing the love of my life, old friend. If you survive that long."

25

JONAH

"What are you all doing here?" I couldn't have come up with a less likely cast of characters if I'd tried. Philippa? Scott? Fane? What had brought all of them together?

My fangs descended the instant my eyes landed on Vance. "Wait. Why is he here?" I was already halfway across the living room before Fane stepped in front of me, holding me back when I tried to get past him.

"It's all right, Jonah. Valerius is dead now. We took care of it."

"It's true," Philippa added, rushing to protect Vance. I should've known she would. "There's a pile of dust in the vault that used to be Valerius. This is Vance."

"And I'm exhausted." Vance offered a weak smile. "It's good to see you. I'm sorry for the trouble you've been through."

I couldn't make sense of anything. "How did you free him? How did this happen?"

"I'll give you the short version," Fane offered. "I found a caster in Duskwood and the same necromancer who first moved Nivia into your mother's body. They performed the spell which placed Valerius back into his body. The necromancer, Elazar, killed him and disappeared."

I stared at my father's face as he told his story and wondered, silently, why he looked slightly different. There was no way to tell exactly where the difference was, but it was there.

Movement on the other side of the room caught my eye. It was Scott, and he was watching me as though he expected something to happen. The intensity of his gaze was disturbing. What was I missing?

Valerius was no longer a threat. That was good to hear—one less menace to be concerned about.

But he wasn't at the forefront of my mind.

"Fane. I have to talk to you." I pulled him aside, into the kitchen.

"What is it? I was just on my way out." His face darkened. "Sirene. Is she well? Where is she? I thought I asked you to—"

"You did, and I did. She's downstairs, in an unused apartment. The baby's here and is well."

He let out a short breath, his eyes wide. "The baby is well? What of Sirene?" He gripped my shoulders, shaking me. "What of Sirene?"

He had never come out and said it, and after that, there was no need to. He loved her. Only a man who truly loved a woman would react the way he had. I would've done the same if it had been Anissa whose life was in danger.

I kept that in mind as I spoke to him. "She survived, but I don't know how much longer she can hold on. She needs a witch to heal her. Too much blood lost, too much... I forget the word Anissa used. She's ill and fading faster."

His eyes lit up. "A witch..." He let go of me and rushed from the kitchen, yelling a name I'd never heard before.

"Branwen."

Who was that? I stepped back into the living room, hoping for some direction. Sirene was dying, and he was calling out a random name. Everyone there seemed to know something I didn't.

He came back from the hall with a small, black-haired woman I'd never seen before. Was this Branwen? She had the same calm, commanding presence Sirene possessed.

"She's a caster and a good friend of Sirene's," Fane explained, nearly dragging her to me. "Branwen, she needs you. The child has come."

"The child?" Philippa asked.

"Where is she?" Branwen looked to me for answers.

"Downstairs. She needs help, right away. She survived the birth earlier tonight but is hanging on by a thread now."

"We must hurry, then."

I led them out of the penthouse, with hope in my heart for the first time since we'd found Sirene's blood back at headquarters.

I forgot I'd gone upstairs to get blood for Anissa and me, I was so relieved to have found help, feeding was the last thing on my mind. I didn't think Anissa would mind going hungry for a little while longer if there was something even more important on the way back with me.

We didn't wait for the elevator, taking the stairs instead. Scott brought up the rear; I hadn't expected him to come with us. If anything, I thought Philippa would have. She must've considered Vance more important.

I couldn't blame her. She hadn't been there for the birth. She didn't have to care. As far as she and Scott and even Gage were concerned, the idea of our father having a child with a witch might still be anathema. They hadn't spent the time with Sirene that I had.

They had never held our baby sister, either.

Anissa must have heard us coming in, because she met us outside the bedroom door. Her eyes flew open wide when she saw Fane.

Something passed between them without either saying a word, something that hinted at a deeper understanding I wasn't privy to.

"She's in here," she whispered, stepping aside.

I waited for Fane to enter before following him.

Sirene tried to lift her head from the pillow when she saw him, but he went to her with his hands held up. "Don't tire yourself. I'm here."

She was radiant, glowing with joy and pride, though she was gravely pale. "You've come. I didn't think you would make it." She peered down at the baby, who slept on her chest. "This is your daughter."

I took Anissa's hand as we watched Fane ever-so-gently lift the baby from Sirene's arms.

"My daughter? A little girl. Have you named her?"

She shook her head. "I wanted to wait for you. Though I did have an idea, but I don't know how you'll feel about it." She glanced at me. "Any of you."

I had an idea—judging from the way Anissa squeezed my hand, I thought she did, too.

"What is it?" Fane stared down at his daughter with such wonder, I couldn't help the lump in my throat. Like a child discovering something for the first time, instead of a man who'd already fathered four. Perhaps that sort of wonder never faded regardless of how many children a person had. The wonder of new life, innocent and pure.

"Elena."

Instead of looking at her, Fane glanced at me with his eyebrows raised.

I shrugged. "It seems to suit her."

He smiled. "It does, doesn't it?" He sat on the edge of the bed, eyes fixed on the baby's face again. Memorizing her. I wondered if he would be part of her life, or if he'd be in and out as he was with us. It was something I hadn't considered before.

"Fane?" Sirene murmured.

The concern on her face and the way her eyes narrowed led me to fear she was in pain or worse. I realized then she was seeing what I had seen. That something was different.

"Hmm?" Only when he glanced up from the baby did his smile fade.

She sighed. "I thought as much. What happened?"

"You could tell so easily?"

She nodded faintly. "I felt it. You and I are now the same."

I almost laughed. The same? What was she trying to say? That he was a warlock? He was different, but not that different.

Except... he didn't deny it.

"Yes," he admitted. "We are, now."

"What?" I whispered.

The room seemed to spin around me. It wasn't possible. Was it? If so, how? Who had done this? It had to be a very powerful creature. Valerius? Had he done it before he died? Just the sort of evil final act he would commit.

I turned to Anissa and expected to see my horror reflected in her face—or at the very least, surprise. There was none. If anything, she looked guilty and avoided my eyes. What was she hiding?

"Sirene, do you have pain now?" Branwen asked, leaning over the bed.

She shook her head. "Jonah and Anissa took such good care of me. I owe them everything. We wouldn't have our beautiful Elena if it weren't for them." Her eyes closed as she finished speaking, a sweet smile still on her face.

Her chest seemed to still.

"Sirene?" Anissa fled to her side.

"There's no time to waste." Branwen stepped forward, arms already raised. "All of you, leave us."

"I want to stay." Fane handed the baby over to me.

I took her and grabbed Anissa's hand, bringing both along with me as we left the room, closing the door behind us.

The silence in the rest of the apartment was deafening, full of uncertainty.

The baby slept deeply, satisfied with herself and exhausted after all the excitement of her first day.

Good thing, because there was a discussion I needed to have with Anissa.

I turned to her. "What do you know about Fane?"

26

FELICITY

"Is anyone out there?"

I couldn't help but whimper in pain as I dragged myself to the bars separating my desolate little cell from the rest of the cells around me. There were so many.

All empty. I was the only prisoner.

I wondered if I should feel honored.

My knee throbbed horribly as I rested my weight on my good leg and craned my neck to look as far up and down the corridor as possible. Just like above, in the throne room and the tunnels zigzagging beneath the mountains, lit torches lined the walls.

There were fewer down here, though. That was the difference. There was almost no light.

"Hello? Please? I need help."

There was simply too much to ask for all at once. Food and drink might have been a good start. I'd had none since my arrival; there was no way to tell how long I had been sitting alone in this cold, dark cell.

After that, I needed assistance with my knee. I might have been able to heal it quickly had I been given the opportunity to clean the wound, assess the damage and apply a tonic or poultice. Unfortunately, even my cloak had been taken away. I had none of the bottles and vials I had brought with me.

It was so swollen, I couldn't bend my leg. So tender, I couldn't apply more than the barest amount of weight. When, I did, the sensation that I was tearing the underlying muscle made me want to scream. There could even have been bits of stone inside. There was no light for me to see by.

I whimpered again, and, this time, it was frustration and helplessness which tore the sound from my throat. No one cared. I might die of a blood infection without any of them checking on me. What was the purpose of this? Why leave me here to die?

Why not get it over with right away, instead?

I couldn't muster the strength to hop on one leg across the cell, small though as it was, to sit on the rock-hard cot in the corner. Sitting on the floor was just as comfortable, sadly.

I slid down, gripping the bars to ease myself slowly as I stretched the injured right leg out in front of me.

Of all the ways I'd envisioned this mission turning out, this was nowhere on the list.

Hunger twisted my stomach in knots as I tipped my head back against the bars. How long would it be before they fed me? Had Garan forgotten I was here? Unlikely. My presence was the reason he would use to start a war, after all.

That didn't mean he had to take care of me or keep me alive. I wasn't to be used as a bargaining chip, at least that wasn't how he'd made it sound. He would spread the word I'd been imprisoned and used that as a way to keep others in line lest they consider committing a similar transgression.

What was the purpose of any of it? Gregor would never find out what happened to Tabitha. I would never see Allonic again. A terrible, deadly war would be waged, and I couldn't even warn my people. All for nothing.

I hung my head as the tears began to flow, tracing hot paths down my dirt-smudged cheeks. There was nothing around me except silence and cold and hopelessness. I had nothing. I would die here, probably fevered and hallucinating as infection caused my body to shut down a little bit at a time.

It couldn't happen soon enough. I had already lost all hope.

I drifted into a light sleep, dreams and images overlapping in my head. There was no pain, only confusion and guilt. The sense that something terrible was coming. Something I was powerless against. And I was very, very small. Insignificant. A single piece of a much larger whole. The sense of desperation was sickening.

The sound of shuffling footsteps jolted me awake.

I lifted my head, craning my neck again to see who was coming, fighting my way into a kneeling position while my right leg stretched out beside me. "Please. Water. Something." My voice was a scratchy croak after I'd spent hours crying out for help to no avail.

The footsteps grew louder until a tall figure became visible. The hooded man walked my way, carrying a tray. Saliva flooded my mouth when I caught the scent of fresh bread. I would eat. I didn't care what it was, so long as it was food.

There was no making out the shade's face, the hood casting his face in deep shadow. I didn't care about that, either. The pain in my leg and the clenching of my empty stomach were more than enough to dominate my attention.

"Thank you," I whispered as he placed the tray on the cot, his back to me. "Is there anything you can give me for my knee? Please, tell Garan I'm afraid it will become infected unless treated right away."

The shade knelt beside me.

I leaned back, scrambling away, dragging my leg. He clamped a hand over my mouth then used his other hand to lower the hood.

My eyes flew open wide, and I understood why he'd covered my mouth. To silence the shriek of utter joy, relief, surprise.

"Don't make a fuss. Stay quiet." Allonic lowered his hand slowly, looking down the corridor to be sure no one had followed.

"Oh, Allonic. I thought... —"

"Here." He handed me a hunk of bread and cup of water. "I'm sorry, they weren't going to bring you more than this. I couldn't risk loading more onto the tray. Someone would have noticed."

I gulped down the water before digging my teeth into the fresh, warm bread. It wasn't much, but to me, it might as well have been a banquet. I closed my eyes, relishing the taste.

"I would've come sooner," he whispered, "but I couldn't risk it. I've been watching, waiting for someone to decide you should eat. Finally, Steward spoke on your behalf to the guards."

"Who's that?" I whispered, still chewing.

"It doesn't matter. He's respected, though. They listen to him. He managed to get this for you then arranged it so I would be the one to deliver it. It's been two days since I learned you were here."

"Two days?"

"And at least another or two since you were locked in. I'm sorry. I wish I could've come sooner."

"It's all right." What I wanted more than anything, my

immediate needs having been taken care of, was him. I wanted him to hold me. I wanted him to assure me everything would be fine, that no one had to die because of my foolishness.

"What did you say about your knee?" He looked at my covered leg.

"I cut it badly on the way here," I explained, telling him about the rough treatment I'd received. "I couldn't do anything about it. They didn't let me clean it. They took away my tonics. It's terribly swollen."

"May I?" he asked, his hand poised above the robe. I nodded, wincing as the mere act of sliding fabric over the throbbing joint sent bolts of pain all through me. His eyes narrowed when he saw the full extent of the damage, muscles jumping in his cheek, nostrils flaring as his breathing grew heavy.

It wasn't a pleasant sight. The knee had torn open, almost down to the bone. The blood had long since stopped running out, but it had crusted along the wound and all over my leg. The swelling was tremendous, making the joint nearly twice the size of my other knee.

"Don't worry," I whispered, trying to lighten to mood. "It only hurts twice as bad as it looks."

"He allowed this." His voice reminded me of the hissing of a snake.

"I need to do something for it," I said. "Maybe you can get your hands on my cloak? All of my tonics are in there. Water would help, of course, and... —"

"No," he replied with a firm shake of his head. "There's no way I could make it back in here. No excuse to bring your cloak—if I could even find where they'd put it. If it still exists. Garan knows you're important. He's already warned me against trying to get you out."

He had obviously gone to a lot of trouble and was risking quite a lot to be with me.

"What can I do, then? An infection has likely begun to develop, and it will spread soon."

He let out a sharp sigh, holding his head in his hands.

Then, he raised his head, his mouth open in surprise as our eyes met.

"Of course. I can't believe I didn't think of it."

"What?" I glanced from him to the corridor. Just in case.

"The one thing they've all held against me throughout my life. The one thing that sets me apart from them—well, the one thing they care about," he amended, and the fact he sounded almost cheerful baffled me.

"What is it?" I demanded.

He pulled up one of his sleeves. "This." His claws extended, reminding me he was part-vampire.

And then, I knew, too. Vampire blood.

He opened a thin line in his arm as he drew one razor-sharp claw across his skin. Blood began to seep out of the cut. "Hold still," he advised, holding the dripping cut over my knee.

I closed my eyes, bracing myself for what was to come. It wouldn't be painless. I was certain of it. And sure enough, as the torn skin began knitting together and the muscle beneath became whole again, a burning sensation spread through my leg. I gritted my teeth against it, determined not to give us away when we were so close to escaping this terrible place.

"Almost finished," he whispered, his mouth close to my ear. His very nearness was almost enough to drive all thoughts of pain from my mind. He was there. He had come for me. I didn't have to doubt him anymore.

When it was over and the burning ceased, I was slow to open my eyes. Afraid of what I might find.

"Remarkable." He smiled, referring to the thin scar running across my kneecap. No swelling. Nothing but dried blood to indicate there had been a recent injury. "Can you move it?"

I could. "It's just a little stiff," I marveled. "Thank you."

He didn't pull away when I threw my arms around his neck. Then, after a mere moment's hesitation, he returned my embrace. That was the best of all.

"I'm so sorry. It's all my fault you're here," he murmured, his breath hot on the nape of my neck.

"How is it your fault? You didn't do this."

"There's no time to explain now. We have to get out of here. There's only one problem."

"What's that?" He helped me to my feet. I was a bit shaky, weak from days without food, but too happy for it to matter. He still cared for me.

"The exits from the cave have all been enchanted. No one without shade blood can leave or return."

No one without shade blood. I smiled up at him—the frown he gave me in return told me he didn't understand yet. "But I have shade blood, don't I? Right now. Thanks to you."

Understanding dawned on his face. "Do you think it will work?"

"I suppose there's only one way to find out. But how will we get out of here, past the guards?" I hoped it would work. It was the only hope I had.

"Don't worry, I've already worked that out. According to the maps, there are two entrances to this section, but only one of them is guarded. There was a cave-in at the other end, long ago, which no one ever thought to clear out. Since the dungeon is so rarely used, I suppose Ressenden considered it a pointless venture."

"Can we get through there?"

"Certainly. I've been working on it." He took me by the hand and held a finger to his lips, peering out from inside the cell before pulling me along behind him.

My heart raced as we ran the path between the empty cells, all of my attention focused on the point where our hands joined.

That was all that mattered. He was here with me, and he had things under control.

I would've followed him anywhere.

27

ALLONIC

I climbed through the opening I'd created in the fallen rubble first, stepping lightly over the large rocks and offering her a hand to help her through.

"If you knew about this, why didn't you just use it to get through to me?" Felicity asked as she followed.

"I wouldn't have had a key to unlock your cell. I considered it, believe me."

"Of course."

Once we were on the other side, in one of the many tunnels running the length and breadth of the mountain, we were in more danger than ever.

"Put this on." I shook out the folded robes I'd left here for her and waited while she slid them on. "Hood up. Hide your hands inside the sleeves."

"How do I look?" she whispered.

"It will do for now. We'll take the closest exit. I hope you're right about the blood fooling the enchantment. Keep your head down as you walk."

I raised my hood to conceal my face and pictured the map

in my head. It was a skill all shades possessed, the ability to recall knowledge at will. Part of our vocation.

Right at the first intersection. Left at the next. Walk to the five-way intersection and take the second tunnel on the right. I had practiced it so many times in my head, had walked it in my mind's eye. The difficult part was keeping my pace stately rather than breaking into a run. The longer we were here, the greater the chance of our discovery.

So far, so good. None of the shades we passed seemed to notice anything amiss. They were busy gossiping, talking about war. I could almost feel Felicity flinching every time the word was mentioned. So, he had told her his plans.

She followed obediently, asking no questions, matching my pace by lengthening her stride. The stiffness in her knee had all but vanished, judging by the smoothness with which she walked. Remembering the horrid condition she'd been in when I found her was almost enough to convince me to take a detour and visit my cousin one last time.

No, better to watch Gregor get the upper hand on him. That would be a true victory.

There it was. The cave entrance. The same one Jonah and Anissa had first used when they came to ShadesRealm.

It led straight to the human world, where moonlight bathed the trees and grass. A relief. We could escape together, without the worry of the sun's harmful rays.

"I'm scared," she breathed, just behind my left elbow.

"Nothing to be afraid of." We were about to reach the cave, where we would be outside the attention of nearly everyone. No one ever used that entrance, the one closest to my chambers.

We only had to get through it, which was what I knew worried her. Would my blood be enough?

I passed through easily, feeling the invisible wall of energy as I pass through it. "Stop," I hissed, turning.

She froze.

"This is it?" she whispered, her face invisible in the hood's shadow.

"Yes. I only wanted to be certain. All right. Come on."

"I'm afraid."

"What's the worst that could happen? We don't have much time."

"It could kill me."

"I doubt it."

"Allonic. He left me in there to die. This could very well kill me. What better way to rid himself of an inconvenient presence? This way, he can claim he had nothing to do with it. I tried to escape and suffered the consequences."

I exhaled. When she put it that way, I could see her point. Garan was just twisted enough to think that way.

"I love you," she whispered. "I need you to know that before I do this. Just in case."

I opened my mouth to tell her I loved her, too, that I had never loved anyone but her and would love her until my dying breath.

I didn't get the chance before she took a step forward.

And into my arms.

"You did it." I held her to me, our hearts hammering wildly, both of us laughing in disbelief. "You made it through."

"We did it." She raised her head, the hood falling back, and I leaned down to kiss her. She wound her arms around my neck, her tears wetting both our faces.

"Stop!"

The moment came to an abrupt halt when the sound of shouts and pounding feet echoed down the length of the cave.

"Hurry." I took her hand and ran out into the woods, frantic for a place to hide. We weren't out of danger yet.

"What about a portal?" she asked as we ran, ducking under low-hanging branches and, jumping over tree roots and brambles.

I'd have coursed if I had not used so much blood to heal her. I was certain I couldn't course, not yet.

"They'll see it. They might be able to come through behind us."

No, we'd have to wait until they gave up the search. There was no telling how long that would take, however. We only had so many hours left before the sun rose.

I could hear them coming from the cave. One moment there was silence, the next there was shouting and the pounding of feet as the invisible energy field was breached again and again.

It was the only entrance into ShadesRealm which allowed one to see through to what was on the other side.

Mostly unused, but not entirely. I had relied too much on that. I should've known every entrance would have more eyes on it than usual, that if we paused on the other side, they'd still be able to see us.

There was no time to go over my many mistakes as we fled deeper into the woods. I stopped momentarily, holding my breath to listen. I couldn't hear them, but that didn't mean anything. Felicity bent at the waist, her free hand on her thigh, breathing heavily.

There was a boulder further ahead, and I pointed to it. She nodded and summoned up her strength to make it the rest of the way there.

"Sit," I urged her once we arrived, helping her get as comfortable as I could. She was too weak for much more hard running.

I peered out from behind the boulder, listening for any sign we'd been followed. I didn't hear any twig snaps or crunching of leaves, but the faint sound of excited voices floated to me on the evening breeze. They were out there, looking for us.

"How long do you think they'll keep searching?" Felicity slumped against the, rock, her eyes closed.

"I don't know. Long enough to say they tried, for sure. But I don't know how long that will be. If we don't hear anything from them in an hour, at most, we'll go to Avellane. I just don't want to run the risk of them seeing the portal and possibly being able to come through."

"I understand," she whispered, exhausted.

I knelt beside her, ready to spring up at any moment. "I'm so sorry for all of this." Her skin was cool to the touch but covered with a thin sheen of perspiration as I ran my hand over her forehead.

"That's the second time you've apologized." She opened her eyes, regarding me in her usual frank manner. "Why? You aren't Garan. You didn't seize me and lock me in a cell. And oh, Allonic..." Tears filled her eyes. "Your mother. I'm terribly sorry. I suppose you know, if they told you how they caught me."

"Yes. I know. I know much more than you do, in fact."

Heaviness settled in my heart as I silently questioned whether she would still love me when I told her the truth of what I'd done.

"Do you? Do you know what happened to Tabitha? That's why I came. That's why Gregor and I first reached out to Garan. He'd been frantic, trying to understand why she never met him outside the entrance to Avellane."

Poor Gregor. I remembered him waiting there, like a

happy child. Living for the fantasy of a happy future with his one true love. I had shattered that fantasy.

"I never would've guessed things could turn out this way." I sat with my back to the rock, one ear still trained on the area around us. "I wouldn't have chosen the course I did, naturally."

"The course you did? Don't tell me you had something to do with it. No. I can't believe that."

I patted her hand, my heart heavier than ever. "Felicity, there are times when we make choices we couldn't possibly anticipate the consequences of. I am responsible for my mother's death, thanks to a series of terrible decisions."

"You can't mean it. I'm sure you're wrong." There was so much faith in her voice, on her face, that it broke my heart even further to shatter her illusions. She regarded me as someone worthy of respect, someone whose judgment was sound, whose motives were always pure.

It was better for her to know the truth before she entangled herself with me any further. She would regret ever thinking or saying she loved me.

I told her about taking Valerius from the dungeons beneath League Headquarters, about keeping him under my control on entering ShadesRealm. The silver cage. How I had intended to use his ancient powers for my own benefit, in an attempt to take what should've been mine all along.

"You see," I muttered, staring up at the stars to avoid the look of disgust I was certain would be on her face, "I've spent my entire life being Other. Not good enough for either side. By rights, I should be in Garan's place. I should be respected, admired. But because of the vampire blood running through me... —"

"It was Valerius who killed Tabitha, then." Her words fell

on my ears like the boulder against which we sat. Heavy. Hard.

"Yes. I didn't know she would go back there. I thought she'd put it behind her once and for all. I never... I never would have." I turned my face away as emotion threatened to overwhelm me.

"And that was why you were so upset when I told you she'd gone back. Of course. I didn't see it at the time. But, Allonic? You didn't know. This Valerius, he's evil. Truly evil. He didn't need to kill her once she released him. He could have simply left. No, it was his wickedness that caused her death. Not you."

"But if I hadn't been so blinded by greed and ambition..."

"It isn't your fault they never accepted you. You didn't see any other way to get what's rightfully yours. I can't blame you for that."

"Oh, come now." I gazed at her, scoffing in spite of myself. "You don't honestly mean to tell me you understand what happened and don't blame me for it."

"I don't blame you." She sat up, rolling onto her knees at my side and taking both of my hands in hers. "Look at me. Listen to me. You could never have known what he was capable of. You couldn't have known she would come back. Otherwise, you wouldn't have locked him in that cage and left him for her. And I've met Garan. I can see why you would want to usurp him. He's dreadful."

I studied her expression, searching for signs she was lying or at least trying to soften the blow. She appeared sincere. Her eyes shone in the moonlight, sparkling with unshed tears but gazing at me with fierce intensity.

"What's rightfully yours has been kept from you throughout your entire life," she went on. "Not just your place of honor within the shade world, but dignity. Respect. None of this has been afforded to you, simply because of who you were born to. It's absurd. Anyone would grow frustrated, even bitter. And they would want more than anything to set matters right, by whatever means necessary."

"You're only saying that because of your feelings for me."

"I am not." She dropped my hands, folding her arms. "I resent that."

"It's the only explanation. I've gone over things again and again, and everything starts from the point where I took Valerius from the dungeon and brought him to ShadesRealm."

"After which time, he did what he did. You did not force him, Allonic." She took my face in her hands. "You must forgive yourself for what happened."

"It doesn't matter if I forgive myself. What about Anissa? Gregor? Sara?"

"They would forgive you, too. I'm certain of it."

"You don't know my sisters."

"I know Gregor. I know he would. He would never hold you responsible, not when you're in so much pain because of it. He knows you loved her."

"I still do."

"And so does he," she replied with a sad smile.

The moon had moved through the sky since we'd first sat down. "They must have given up," I surmised, looking out from behind the boulder. "We should leave."

"We have to go warn Gregor," she agreed. "Oh, I wish you could've overthrown that Garan. You would've avoided the war that's coming."

The war that was coming. "There might still be a way," I decided. "But we have to go. Now."

Moments later, she created a portal.

I reached for her, and she took my hand with a smile.

"I do love you," she whispered.

"Still?" I asked, awed.

She nodded. "And always."

My heart swelled. So, it was possible to love someone after they admitted the worst thing they had ever done, something which had led to untold pain for many others.

"I love you," I replied before we stepped through the portal together.

28

ANISSA

"Wait a second." Scott joined us, pointedly avoiding having to look at the baby.

So, he hadn't come around yet. That made me sad for him, and for Fane. I had hoped so much the two of them might find a way to connect.

"I don't recall asking you anything," Jonah muttered.

"Let him speak," I urged.

"Why? Because he's about to defend you?"

"No!" I hissed, glancing at the baby. The last thing I needed was to wake her, no matter how Jonah made me want to scream my head off. "Because there's nothing to defend, for starters. Why do you assume I have anything to defend myself over?"

"Because you looked guilty as anything back there, when he admitted he's changed. You knew all along, didn't you? But you didn't say a word."

"Hmm. Let me think back. I seem to remember something else happening in the last day or so. What was it...?" I tilted my head to the side, tapping my chin. "Oh, of course. You're holding her."

"It's no excuse. You could've told me in Avellane."

Scott threw an arm between us, forcing me to take a step back. "Fane didn't want anyone to know. Not Sirene, not you or Philippa. Did you ever think he might want to tell you himself? Or that he knew it would upset Sirene if she knew, and he didn't want to upset her?"

"Why would it upset her?" Jonah glanced from him to me. "It means there's no barrier between them anymore. I'd think that would make her happy."

I faced Scott. "It's not that simple."

"Is anything ever?" Jonah turned away, walking the baby back and forth until she started shifting and fussing in his arms. As though she could sense what was going on around her. She seemed to enjoy being gently bounced, which was what Jonah started to do as he continued to glare at me. "What am I missing?"

"You should put the baby down," I whispered. If he wanted to know the truth, he would get the full truth. Fane lying there on the stone floor, dying…

"Don't tell me what I need to do. What am I missing?"

"He was wounded." It wasn't me who broke the news; it was Scott. "I begged Elazar to save him. It was either that or let him die there."

"A battle," I murmured, still eyeing him and the baby.

"I guess I was too stupid to imagine Elazar would do something like this. I didn't even know it was possible for him to take away Dad's—Fane's—essence and give him a new one. I'm no happier about it than you are. I hate it. It disgusts me."

"Scott," I whispered.

It sounded as though I was chiding him, and maybe I was. His bigotry had no place in the story, whether he believed it did or not.

"It's true. I don't care that I'm supposed to be all right with this. I'm still not. He's not my father anymore—he hasn't been for decades, but it had never been this bad before. I could've accepted him back into my life if it weren't for this."

"All right, all right. I don't know how much more of this I can hear," Jonah grumbled.

"Like you don't know what I'm talking about. Like you haven't felt the same."

"I'm not saying I haven't, but things have changed. I've changed. I'm not so stubborn that I can't admit when I was wrong."

They stared at each other, and I could've sworn electricity crackled in the air between them. I wouldn't have blamed Scott if he'd accused Jonah of sounding sanctimonious; he did, even though he was also right.

"It's not Fane's fault," I reminded Scott. "Not that there is any fault in being a warlock. But as you said, he would've died."

"Maybe he should have."

"Enough!"

The baby wailed in response to Jonah's barked command.

I jumped, but Scott only shrugged and walked away, going to the windows and staring out. But he didn't leave. He could have but didn't.

I went to Jonah, reaching for the baby. He handed her to me, probably grateful to pass her off while she was crying.

"She's probably hungry," I guessed.

Jonah nodded, too distracted to notice or even care very much at the moment. "He almost died?"

I wanted more than anything to hold him and take away his pain, confusion, whatever it was. "He did. It was very close. The battle... it was terrible."

He glared down at me—eyes narrowed, jaw tightening. I knew that look and braced myself for what was coming. "You could've told me. You had the opportunity to tell me when you told me what happened back there on the island. But you didn't. You deliberately left it out."

And there it was. What I had dreaded but knew was on its way all along. It was a choice I made, wasn't it? To lie for Fane. "I have to get her a bottle," I announced, going to the kitchen instead of getting deeper into a fight.

He followed me. "You owe me more than this."

I pulled a bottle from the refrigerator. "More than what?"

"More than lying to me."

"I did not lie. Don't accuse me of something I didn't do."

"It was a lie of omission."

It wasn't easy, verbally sparring with him while trying to recall how Mom took care of Sara when she was an infant. The formula couldn't be cold, could it? I'd have to warm it somehow, maybe under a hot tap. "Be as angry as you want about this, but it doesn't make what you're saying the truth. Your father ordered me not to say a word."

"He ordered you?" Jonah scoffed. "Since when do you follow his orders?"

I turned my head away from the sink, staring at him. "Since when do I follow yours?"

He flinched. "I never said you did. You're twisting my words around."

"Am I?" I tested the bottle before inserting the rubber nipple into the baby's mouth. She latched on quickly, almost greedily. "It doesn't matter or change anything. I followed his wishes. There. Does that sound better?"

"Don't do that."

"Then don't presume to tell me what I must or mustn't tell you," I snapped. "I used my discretion. I'm sorry if that's such a problem for you. He didn't want me to tell you because it would've meant telling you the entire story. Scott wasn't exaggerating. Fane had only moments left. Moments. It was…"

It was too much, was what it was. All of it. The sick rush of memory, the helplessness. Watching him slip away. Knowing Jonah would lose him again, because he had fought to free me and Scott.

"Do you remember what it was like in there?" I tipped my head in the general direction of the bedroom. We hadn't heard a sound coming from inside yet. I wondered if that boded well or not. "Weren't there moments when you felt responsible to Sirene? *For* her? And to Fane, as well? Like you had to save her for his sake? And the baby's? And do you remember how helpless and frustrated and sick it made you feel when she started to slip out of consciousness, and neither of us knew whether it meant she was about to die? Weren't there at least a few times when you told yourself you'd do anything to keep her alive?"

He didn't need to answer, and the expression on his face told me I didn't need to go on. He understood. When he spoke again, his voice was softer than before. "And the necromancer did it to him? Fane mentioned the name upstairs. Elazar."

"Yes. He tricked Scott; but Scott was desperate, too. Frantic, panicking. Your father was dying in front of us. What else was he supposed to do when someone approached and offered to save him?"

"He should've been smarter."

"Jonah, stop being so stubborn for once," I snapped, not caring if the baby fussed or not. "I swear, you're all alike. All of you. You got on Scott's case just a few minutes ago for being so hardheaded, didn't you? And now, you do the same thing. If you're not willing to put yourself in his shoes, I'll do it for you."

"What do you mean?"

"I mean you would've agreed if it meant saving your father. No matter how much discomfort or misunderstanding is still between you, you would've agreed to Elazar's terms. You might have asked him what those terms were before sending your father off with him, but you would've agreed. If you hadn't, and he had died, you would have blamed yourself. You would've asked yourself for the rest of your life if you should've chosen differently. And you wouldn't have been able to face your brothers and sister because of it."

I sounded harsh, cold, even to my own ears, but he needed to hear it. His face went blank as he let my words sink in, while I held my breath in the hope he'd come around.

In the blink of an eye, his features hardened again. "You know something? That doesn't matter right now. That's not even the subject at hand. The subject is you are continually leaving me out of important matters."

"Such as?" I rolled my eyes and sighed.

"Besides this, you mean? Let's talk about Ressenden. You killed him, but you never bothered to mention even wounding him."

"It was self-defense. Should we discuss everything the two of us have done in self-defense? Because I'm sure you'd have a few stories to tell, as well. But I've learned already it's a fool's errand, going after the absolute truth. What is that, anyway? Our lives aren't simple. I can't sit down at the end of every day and recite a journal entry for you, and I don't expect you to do the same for me. As it is, I don't even think you and I were together when I threw that blade at Ressenden. It's all a blur at this point."

"All right. That's true. If we weren't together at that time,

I can see how I didn't know. Going forward, I would appreciate a little truth. I don't like being the last to know about things that are important. And Fane is important. What happened to him is important."

I opened my mouth to sling another argument his way but knew at the last second it was no use. My shoulders sagged. "I'm so tired of fighting about this same issue again and again, Jonah. If you have a problem with Fane not wanting you or anyone else to know before he was ready for you to know, take it up with him. I can't do this anymore."

The creak of the bedroom door opening sent us both out of the kitchen.

As Fane stepped out of the room, his eyes immediately swept the area, looking for his daughter. He might not even have known he was doing it.

"Here." I offered her to him. "How is she?"

"She'll be all right." He exhaled. "She'll be all right. Branwen..." He shrugged. "Sirene will live."

The last of the tension I'd been holding in my body dissolved, and I found myself leaning against him for a moment while I took hold of myself. She would live. Her baby would have a mother's protection. I hadn't known how deeply afraid I'd been for the poor child until that very second.

"It's all because of you two," Fane continued, turning toward Jonah. "She never could've gotten through it alone, and you took excellent care of her. I could never thank you enough. You don't know how remarkable it is that she made it through. It wasn't supposed to happen. It's rare that it did."

I couldn't help but wonder why that was. Yes, the birth had been brutal, but many were. Was it simply because the women giving birth to hybrids were so often left alone? Or did she happen to be stronger than most? Was there some type of chemistry I didn't understand?

"I'm so glad. We both are." I glanced at Jonah, who nodded. He was still angry with me—I knew better than to expect him to get over things quickly—but he was as happy as I was, too. Baby Elena would have her mother. She had a fighting chance.

Scott was still on the far side of the apartment, staring out the window. He hadn't moved, not even when Fane made his announcement. Fane saw him there, and a bit of the light left his eyes.

"At least it's possible for me to have a relationship with one of my sons," he murmured. "It's possible."

Was it? I wouldn't have questioned him for the world, not when he was so hopeful, but I had my doubts. Jonah wanted his father's love and guidance, something he didn't have to explain for me to understand, but he still had doubts. There was still so much standing in their way.

Then, I remembered watching him feed Elena for the first time. His anxiousness, wondering if she was getting enough food. His caution with her. The way he looked at her. The way he'd fought alongside me to bring her into the world and keep her mother alive.

There was hope for him. For both of them. I had to believe it.

29

JONAH

Scott was still staring out the window when I went to him. A pang of guilt caught me as I did. I had forgotten all about him for so long. Too wrapped up in Anissa, Fane, the clan, and the league. He had Sara, I'd told myself, and the two of them could take care of each other.

I was wrong.

"Not impressed with the baby?" I muttered, standing beside him.

We didn't face each other, but we rather looked out over the city. It was early morning, the specially treated windows allowing us the luxury of enjoying early morning sunlight. Granted, the color was off. Tinted darker than it naturally would've been. But it kept us unharmed.

"I've never been very impressed with babies in general," he replied, sounding bored.

"What are you thinking about over here?"

"A lot of things."

So that was the game we were playing. I would have to draw everything out of him—even then, I'd get a sentence at a time. I bit the side of my tongue to hold back a reminder of how busy I was, and how little time I had to waste with his childishness. That was the last thing he needed, and probably something I had yelled at Gage, once, some time ago. We all knew how well that had gone.

"Anissa told me what happened on Shadowsbane." I reported this as casually as though I were commenting on the cloudy horizon, when, really, it looked as though a storm was on its way. Coming toward us.

My brother scoffed. "I know. I heard. You two aren't exactly quiet when you start arguing."

"I would've done the same thing." I watched his reflection, gauging his reaction. "I just wanted to tell you that. You did what I would've done."

His face remained blank, untouched. "You would've been smarter."

"I don't know about that. How can a person be smart when they're watching their father die? It would've torn me apart."

"Yes, well, I made my decision. And look where it got him. All that mattered to me at the moment was saving him. I never thought about what it might mean, how it might change him. I didn't know who I was dealing with."

"Is that what's getting to you about this? It doesn't seem to me he's suffering in the least. He's happy right now, Scott. Look at him." I glanced over my shoulder, to where he was seated with the baby in his arms.

Anissa sat beside him, feet drawn up under her legs, explaining the feeding schedule we'd already set and how good a baby Elena seemed to be. How very unique.

My brother remained still. "I'd rather not." Disgust was plain in his voice.

"Do you really mean to tell me that if someone had

warned you what Elazar would do to save his life, you would've refused? Do you honestly mean that?"

His silence chilled me worse than any explanation could have.

There was no getting through to him. I was wasting my time. The last thing either of us needed was for me to drive a wedge between us by pressing him too hard. I had learned the hard way, with Gage, about the dangers of doing that.

"I'm going to leave," he announced, still staring out over the skyline.

"Good idea. Go up, get some rest, feed. Maybe get a shower; you've been doing a lot of traveling," I added with a chuckle, hoping to lighten the mood.

"I don't mean leaving to go upstairs. I mean leaving for good. Or, at least, for a while." He finally moved, turning his head just enough that our eyes met. Challenging me to forbid him?

That was my instinct, of course. To forbid him. I was head of the family, the clan, even interim leader of the league. As such, it was my responsibility to keep the members of my family in line. I had every right to insinuate myself in his business.

But that wasn't really the case, and we both knew it. He was well past adulthood and could make his own choices.

"Where will you go?" I whispered, striving to keep our conversation private. I hadn't guessed it would take the turn it had.

"I don't know yet," he admitted. "I mean, I have the entire world out in front of me. I could go just about anywhere there are those of our kind."

"Is it because of Fane and the baby?" I wouldn't call her by the name Sirene had given her. I wouldn't twist the knife in his heart. It was difficult enough for me to think of her as Elena and remember my mother. While I recognized it as the kind, thoughtful gesture Sirene had intended it to be, I also recognized how easy it would be for my brother to misconstrue it.

He shook his head, frowning. "No. At least, not entirely. There's so much more."

"Like what? You can tell me. I want to help if I can."

"I don't know that there's anyone who can help me but me," he admitted, shrugging. "It sounds crazy. I know it does. But I talked to the necromancer. I know, I know," he said, holding a hand up to stop me when my mouth fell open. "He didn't give me advice, if that's what you're worried about."

"What did he tell you?"

"He accused me of being sheltered. Of not knowing the world. He said Sara's betrayal wouldn't have hurt as deeply as it did if I had a little perspective, a little more experience. It got me thinking. What if he's right? I've spent my entire life living with the family, within the clan. That's all that's ever existed for me." His eyes darkened. "And you all kept things from me. You didn't tell me he was alive, for one."

"You're right. We didn't," I agreed somberly.

"Why?"

"I don't know why. I suppose… it was all so complicated, and the fewer of us who knew about it, the better."

"Do you know how that made me feel? Like I didn't matter." He shrugged. "Well, maybe I didn't. Not enough to be brought into the inner circle. I understand."

"Don't make it about that. It wasn't personal."

"It was to me. Again, though, it's over. Now that there's no war with the Carvers—not at the moment, with Marcus being locked up—I feel like there's breathing room enough for me to get out. See some of what's out there. Maybe have something for myself."

Funny how even though I knew it would be wrong to argue his decision, the urge to keep him with us still pulled at me. He was my younger brother. It was in my blood to want to protect him. But he wasn't a child, and he clearly needed to get some perspective on what was outside our clan. I was still embarrassed for him, remembering what Anissa told me he'd done on Shadowsbane. And what had been done to him as a result.

"I know better than to fight," I murmured with a shrug. "I made that mistake with Gage and look where it got us. I won't do that again."

"Is that your way of telling me it's all right to go? Because I wasn't asking for permission."

"And I'm not granting it," I replied with a thin smile. "I'm merely letting you know you won't face any opposition from me. Anything I can do to help you, I'm happy to do."

"Thank you." He glanced over in the direction of the sofa, where Fane was still wrapped around his daughter's little finger.

I winced on his behalf, watching our father fall deeper in love with his new baby.

"I think I'll be leaving soon. As in tonight. As soon as it's safe to leave."

"Understood." I cleared my throat to get everyone's attention, then stared pointedly at my brother. If he wanted to do what he was about to do, it was up to him to announce it.

After shooting me a dirty look, he said, "I just told Jonah I've decided to leave for a while. I don't know how long. I don't know where I'll go. But I need to."

Anissa's eyes widened, and she gawped at me. But she seemed to understand. She should've by this point, having seen so much more than I had.

Fane, however, didn't seem to. "Why would you do this, when you're safe here?"

Scott raised his chin. "Not that I have to explain myself to you, but sometimes being safe isn't all that matters. I've been safe for most of my life. Look where it's gotten me. I wonder if anyone would've noticed I was gone if I hadn't announced my leaving."

"We would've noticed," Anissa assured him with a faint smile. "Scott, we would have."

"That's very nice of you to say, but you'll excuse me if I have a hard time believing it."

"Scott." Fane handed the baby to Anissa before standing. "Please, be careful. Whatever you do, wherever you go, know that I'll do anything in my power to help you. We have friends everywhere, throughout the various realms which comprise our world. One of them can get word to me if you're in trouble. Please." He took a chance and raised his hands, bringing them to Scott's shoulders. "Please. Don't let your pride get in the way. If you need my help, call on me. I'll come running."

Scott shifted in discomfort, clearly unimpressed by this. "You don't..."

"I mean it." His fingers tightened. "Son. I mean it."

"All right," Scott agreed. "I'll keep that in mind. Thank you." It was as close to a reconciliation as either of them were capable of, even if Scott couldn't have gotten away from Fane fast enough.

"You're leaving right away?" Anissa asked.

"Tonight, at sunset. I'll have time to pack and get myself together."

"And you'll at least be able to say goodbye to Philippa," she offered.

He only snorted. "If she's not too busy with Vance. Which

I'm sure she is. I doubt she would notice if I took off again. But I get it. She has something in her life. Somebody."

Somebody. He didn't even have that.

Anissa averted her eyes, obviously uncomfortable at the veiled reference to her sister. It was enough to make me wonder exactly what had changed in Sara's heart. I found myself wanting to spend a few minutes with her. Maybe more than a few. She had destroyed my brother, something I didn't take lightly.

He left without another word, without so much as a glance at our sister. I wished there was something I could say to make things right. To at least ease whatever weighed on his mind.

"His battles aren't yours to fight," Fane reminded me.

"Then why do I feel like they are?" I sighed, staring at the door Scott had just walked through.

He chuckled. "Because you're a leader, and leaders tend to take on the burdens of those they lead. It's something we all have in common once we step into positions of power—those of us who take our positions seriously. I can't imagine Lucian ever caring about the problems of those closest to him."

"Or Marcus," Anissa muttered, shuddering.

The mention of his name brought me back to reality. There was still so much to be settled, including the matter of the two prisoners being held in the dungeons, and the guards I still barely trusted.

In addition to the man my sister was in love with, who, as far as the league was concerned, had killed his father. And now Vance was free.

Not to mention the fiancée who only seemed to trust me when it was convenient for her.

30

MICAH

"It's good, being out here with you," I said as Cari and I stalked through the park together. "And on such a beautiful night as this."

"It is a beautiful night," she agreed, and I naturally noted the way she didn't share the original sentiment. She was being very careful with her words as of late.

Something was wrong.

I used every last bit of control in my possession to keep from pressing her for an explanation. She would pull even further away if I did, and for nothing. There was no room for paranoia. It would only ruin what I had worked so hard to build between us.

"Are you feeling well?" I asked, keeping my tone light.

"Oh, yes. Is it possible for those of our kind to not feel well?" She grinned. "There's still so much I don't know, of course."

That was much more like it. Her light sense of humor, her intelligence. What I liked best about her, aside from the beauty which only seemed to grow by the day. Gage had done a great thing by turning her, perhaps the smartest act of his entire life.

"Well, I can share a secret with you," I murmured, glancing back and forth as though looking for eavesdroppers.

She giggled. "What is it?"

"You have a very, very long time in which to figure it all out."

Her laughter was like the tinkling of bells. "It feels as though I've been like this forever already."

"Oh, *ma cherie*." I linked my arm with hers as though we were two sweethearts on a stroll through the park on a lovely evening, "your understanding of time will change greatly as the years roll on. I promise you that."

"And you're never one to break a promise." She smiled in return.

My own smile faltered slightly before I could stop it. What was she driving at? It sounded like a perfectly innocent statement on the surface. Anyone who'd heard it would've assumed she was being sincere.

I wasn't so certain.

Was I driving myself mad? Was this all in my head? It had been so very long since I'd met anyone even close to my level of intelligence. It had been my main weapon for much of my time in Paris, the thing which had kept me alive in the early days. Before I'd established a place for myself.

We passed a lit fountain, water spraying high into the air. The droplets resembled jewels, lit as they were. Several couples stopped to enjoy the sight. We stopped, too. Anyone would think we were just like them as we stood with our arms linked.

I watched her from the corner of my eye. There was no way she knew anything. I was fooling myself into seeing things which simply didn't exist, and I knew better than to let my imagination run away with me. At least, I had always been before.

"Do you see anyone you enjoy?" I murmured, leaning in close as though I were whispering something sweet in her ear.

She smelled so lovely. I couldn't help lingering there.

Until she pulled away with a light laugh, as though she were teasing. "Maybe. Maybe."

"Who?" I asked, endeavoring to keep the mood easy. Why did she pull away from me? Why did she still resist? It had been two weeks. She was no closer to being mine than she'd been while Gage had been in the picture.

What was it about him that made him so impossible for her to forget?

"There's a girl walking past, on the other side of the fountain," she murmured, her eyes shifting in the direction of the girl she described.

I followed her gaze and saw who she referred to.

"You have a good eye." I smiled.

The two of us began walking in her direction, making sure to keep our pace leisurely but deliberate.

"I thought you knew that by now." She chuckled. "You always manage to make it sound as though you're surprised."

"I suppose it's still a surprise you've taken to this life so quickly."

"I wouldn't say I've quite taken to it entirely," she murmured, the two of us speeding up as we followed the short, dark-haired girl deeper into the park.

"What does that mean?"

"This still makes me uncomfortable on some level. Taking advantage of someone who doesn't know what's about to hit them. Using the things I know against them without their knowledge. It's unfair. I wish it didn't have to be this way."

"Think of it as survival," I whispered, my consciousness

beginning to fade away as I focused on the meal in front of me. She was plump, fairly glowing with good health, and I imagined there being more than enough for the two of us to share. An appetizer of sorts, before we both chose an entrée to enjoy on our own.

"Survival," Cari repeated.

"Yes. It's either you or them." The thirst began overtaking me, my senses beginning to pinpoint, completely focused on the task at hand—luring the girl, overtaking her, draining her.

"You're right," Cari whispered, as though she were very far away; she could've been on the moon, even though we were still touching. "It's all a matter of survival. Thank you for making this so much easier for me. I'll never cease being grateful to you for that."

I didn't care much at that moment about her gratitude. I wanted to feed.

"I'll even give you this one all to yourself. My gift to you," she whispered.

It was exactly the right thing to say. I released Cari's arm and caught up with the girl, smiling at her just before I clamped a hand over her mouth and ducked behind a tall hedge. She never stood a chance, poor thing.

I drank deep, drank until her weak struggles ceased. It was like being born again. Every single time, like being reborn. Drinking in the very essence of another being, their vitality, their energy.

Everything sharpened, came into clearer focus. The cool night air on my skin, the way it ruffled my hair, the softness of her body as it slid to the ground, crumpling in a ball at my feet.

The sting of silver at my throat.

"Now that you've finished," Cari hissed in my ear, the

blade hovering just over my skin after the first startling contact, "I would appreciate your being so kind as to tell me where you're holding Gage."

31

CARI

My hands shook inside the gloves I'd slid on while Micah was feeding, but I never lost my grip on the knife. It was a matter of life or death, and I didn't intend to lose.

He let out a sharp laugh of disbelief. "What is all this? A joke? I don't find it very amusing."

"You know what I don't find amusing, Micah?" I whispered, tapping his throat with the blade and delighting in the way he jumped when it made contact. "I don't find it very amusing that you had Gage taken away and blamed it on the league. I don't appreciate that you've been lying to me all this time. I hate what you've done. But you're going to tell the truth now because, otherwise, I'll slit your throat with this knife. How does that sound?"

His powerful body tensed in front of me, pressed against mine. "It sounds as though you're bluffing."

"Am I?" I touched him again, this time more than a mere tap.

He jumped, gasping in pain.

"Now, now," I chided. "Be careful with the sudden movements. I wouldn't want to do something we'll both regret."

"Where did you find a silver knife?"

It was a stall tactic, but I didn't mind. "You'll appreciate the poetry of this," I murmured with a smile, my breath stirring the hair at the back of his neck. "I found it in an antique store. It's roughly as old as you. Don't you find that fascinating? Both of you are so old, and yet you look as good as new."

"That is rather poetic," he murmured with a dry chuckle.

"By the way, here's something I do appreciate, the way you're doing your damnedest to placate me. To make me believe we're friends. To share a joke with me. I'm not in a joking mood, and I see through all of your tactics now. I can't believe I was ever so blind."

"What is this all about? You think I have something to do with Gage's disappearance?" He was breathing faster than normal, trying hard to pretend he was in control though we both knew he wasn't.

I could practically see the wheels turning in his head as he weighed his options. There were none, of course, but he didn't know that. The fool.

"I know you do. I know you had him taken from me because you're selfish and evil. All you want is what you want. It doesn't matter what others want, or what happens to them once you've grown tired or bored. You only think about yourself. Isn't that right?"

"You think you know me," he whispered, freezing again when the knife tapped his throat.

I might have enjoyed that a little bit too much, but I reminded myself it was nothing compared to what Naomi had described as starvation. What Gage was going through.

The memory of this got me back on track. I didn't want to prolong his pain. It was bad enough I'd had to wait an entire two days since Naomi came clean to enact my revenge —one night to get out and find the knife, then this night. But it wouldn't be much longer.

I'm coming, Gage. I swear.

"I do know you," I whispered, cooing in his ear the way he'd done to me in his clumsy attempts at seduction. "Someone told me everything I needed to know. All I have to do is confirm you've left Gage in that old prison outside the city. The one you used before."

He let out a sharp laugh. "You can't be serious."

I let the blade touch his throat, harder this time, and longer. His skin sizzled. He gritted his teeth against the pain but couldn't hold back a groan. "I'm very serious. Stop wasting my time, or I'll end your worthless life here and now. Don't test me, Micah. I'm still young and strong. Do you think you stand a chance? Truly? When you know how desperate I am?"

"Even if he was in a prison," Micah began, his voice a little shakier than I'd ever heard it, "how in the world do you think you could ever get him out? Magic? Or perhaps this super strength you just alluded to would be enough to break iron bars."

"I don't need iron bars." I released him, and he staggered forward with a gasp of surprise, one hand over his throat when he whirled on me.

His eyes bulged when he recognized the skeleton key I held up.

"Where... where did you get that?" he demanded, eyes still wide with shock.

The explanation was simple. "Naomi gave it to me."

"No! She would never do that. What reason would she have?"

"It's simple, Micah," Naomi said as she stepped out from

behind a tree a few yards away. "I did it for myself. And for Xavier."

He gaped at her. "How dare you? Are you insane?"

"No." She smiled and shook her head. "I'm very sane. Finally, I'm sane. I always knew what you did to him, though I didn't want to believe it. I had myself fooled into believing I needed you more than I loved him. That's just not true. He didn't deserve what you did to him, just like Gage doesn't deserve what he's currently suffering through."

"You don't know what you're talking about." He whirled on me, eyes wide. "She's never been reliable. Always had emotional issues. I've kept her close to my side for decades because I didn't trust what she would do outside my supervision."

"Spare me your lies," I murmured, still wielding my knife. I took a jab at him with it and delighted in the way he flinched away. "I know where he is, and I'm going to get him now. And you'll have the knowledge that your plans didn't turn out the way you wanted. Not this time."

"You will not leave me. This is outrageous. What do you think you'll be able to do on your own, with no protection?"

"Honestly?" I asked, tilting my head to the side as I considered this. "It's a good question. What will we do without protection? The way I see it, we can't do much worse than we did with you."

"If he's even still alive," Micah spat.

Just like that, the mask dropped, revealing who he truly was. He worked hard on that façade of his. It was bound to fail sometime, I guessed.

"I would tell you, you should hope he is, or else, but…" I looked around as one by one, more clan members trickled in from the darkness. "Well, I think you've got bigger problems than that right now."

He looked around, eyes wide and wild. "I'm glad you're here. Look what they're doing to me. Help me! Restrain them!"

Naomi and I exchanged a glance, then laughed. But it was a bittersweet moment. Neither of us particularly rejoiced in what was happening—still, it was a victory to watch Micah crumble. And sort of pathetic that he thought his clan was there to help him.

"Micah, Micah, Micah," Naomi murmured. "Do you think they've come to protect you? Do you honestly believe you deserve protection after what you've done?"

He blinked, then looked around again as a dozen of the vampires I had gotten to know since arriving in Paris surrounded him. "You told them your lies? You spread your vile stories about me?"

"Enough," she replied, cutting him off with a sharp glare. "Enough of this. It's all over for you. They know what you've done, what you did so long ago. To a member of your own clan, and then to your oldest friend. This is unforgivable. We might be outside the league's jurisdiction, but we have our own laws. Laws of which you're well aware."

He glanced from one of them to the other, wordlessly. It wouldn't come. He was beyond help, anyway, and through no one's fault but his own. He had dug his own grave.

Naomi shifted her gaze from him to me, tossing the backpack my way. I caught it deftly. We exchanged a long, meaningful look.

"Go. Hurry. Don't worry about what happens here."

"Naomi..."

"I know," she whispered, nodding, a single tear running down her cheek. "Make it right, now. You can. There's still time."

"Thank you. Thank all of you." I turned away. I couldn't see what was about to happen.

He deserves this. He has this coming to him for everything he's done. He's hurt so many people. He made his choices.

Everything Naomi had told me before I left for the hunt with Micah ran through my head as I turned my back on him.

"Cari!" Micah's voice was little more than a whisper as I hurried away, tears in my eyes.

The last thing I heard before coursing in the direction of the old prison was the snarl of a dozen vampires descending on their prey.

32

GAGE

I pried my eyes open when the rat who tugged at the hem of my pants got a little too forceful.

But I couldn't muster the strength to shake him off. I tried. I did. But he knew I wasn't really going to stop him. They'd all grown bolder as I'd deteriorated. I could only moan in mind-bending agony as they danced around me, waiting for the chance to begin their feast.

They would start soon. And I would have no choice but to kill them and have a feast of my own.

I needed to feed. I would be forgiven for taking such drastic steps. I had to be. Didn't I? Anyone in my position would do the same. They would drink if it meant an end to the agony. There was a never-ending supply of them running in and out all the time. I didn't need to starve. I didn't need to suffer.

"Get. Off." I growled with all the strength I had, in spite of the pain in my throat and my head and all through my body. "Get off me!" I jerked my leg, and the little beast went flying.

But he wouldn't stay away for long.

"Please… let me die…" I moaned, my head rolling from side to side as I lost my already weak grasp on sanity. It would leave me entirely, and soon. I would begin dining on rats and spiders, and that would be it. I would be gone forever.

Even if Cari ever found me, what would she find? And perhaps that was how Micah wanted it. He'd wait until I was so far gone as to be unrecognizable then bring her to me.

Would I even know her?

I swallowed, wincing as fire raced down my dry throat. Just a drop of blood. Just a single drop. I found myself looking down at my wrist, pondering the idea…

"Gage!"

My head snapped upward, the pain ringing out but less sharply than before because that was her voice.

But no. I had to be imagining it. Just as I'd been doing for days on end.

"Gage! Where are you?"

Feet pounded the floor as someone ran through the place, feet I imagined.

It couldn't be true. Just another cruel trick my broken brain was playing on me. I couldn't be bothered.

Perhaps I should bite into my wrist after all…

"Gage! Just tell me where you are!"

The footsteps grew louder, as did the voice that sounded so much like Cari's. A voice with an edge of panic in it.

Panic?

Panicked. As though she was looking for me.

"Cari?" I croaked. Even I could barely hear myself. I swallowed, squeezing my eyes shut and summoning every last bit of strength. *It's now or never.* "Cari!"

Silence. The running stopped. In that instant, my heart dropped. Then, "Gage! I'm here! I'm coming!"

It couldn't be true. It wasn't possible. It was the most vivid hallucination of all. That was the only explanation.

"Gage! Gage!" She ran up to the bars, holding them in her hands. "Oh, Gage, my God, Gage!"

I blinked hard. "It's you?" I rasped, still unwilling to allow myself to hope.

"It's me! Hold on!"

Her hands shook violently as she reached around in the pocket of her jeans, searching for something. She dropped the key the first time she inserted it into the lock but managed to turn it and swing the door open on the second try.

"Gage. My love, my love." She came to me, dropping to her knees at my side. "My love. What's he done to you?"

"Cari?" I reached for her with one filthy hand then pulled back. I didn't want to dirty her.

She didn't care. "I'm real. I'm real, and I'm here, and you're going to get out of this terrible place." She took my wrist and guided my hand to her cheek. "See? I'm real."

I broke down, my head falling forward, shoulders shaking. She cried holding me, but only for a minute before jumping to her feet.

"I brought you something." She sprinted off before I could beg her not to leave me.

I was struck with the sudden fear she might never come back, that something might happen to her along the way. The ultimate cruelty, losing her when I'd just gotten her back.

But she did return, and this time it was with a body slung across her shoulders. She was still so strong.

"Here. I dazed him around a half-mile ago. A hitchhiker." She dropped him at my side. A young man, eyes closed.

The pulse still throbbed in the side of his neck.

I fell on him, my fangs opening the artery before I took

the blood faster than the heart could pump it to my lips. It was glorious, a miracle. Life passing through my lips and down my throat and through my body.

I shuddered in pleasure and relief as I finished, raising my head and meeting Cari's concerned gaze.

"My love," she sighed, pink tears still flowing. It was all she needed to say. The expression on her face told me the rest.

"It's not enough, I'm afraid," I whispered, my voice already stronger.

"I'm sure, but I could only carry one at a time," she replied, apologetic.

"Don't worry. I'm sure we'll find another." I stood, slowly, leaning on the wall for support. My legs seemed strong enough to support me. The pain was already fading to nothing but a memory.

A memory I wanted to never relive. Not for anything.

"How did you find me?"

"It's a long story. I think we should get out of here, first." Cari looked around as though she was waiting for someone to discover us.

"Where is he?" I asked, thinking I recognized her apprehension for what it was.

"He won't be bothering us anymore. At least, I don't think so. But I'm not thrilled with the idea of being here any longer than we need to. You don't ever have to see this terrible place again."

"Where is he?" I demanded, though my voice was still soft.

I wasn't about to take a step from that cell without knowing exactly who or what I was going to face outside.

She grimaced. "I don't know. In the city. Dead, most likely, or dying. It was Naomi who helped me. He's done this before. To someone she loved. She finally betrayed him and made it possible for me to get away. She even stole his key to the cell."

"And him?" I didn't want to speak his name, not ever again.

"They're dealing with him the way someone who's done what he did should be dealt with. I didn't want to stay around to watch. Though nothing would've given me more pleasure than seeing his worthless life end, I had more important things to worry about." She took my hand. "Come on. I can answer any questions you may have later."

She was right. It was time to leave. I walked out of the cell, noticing the rats scurrying along the walls and in the corners. They watched as we walked down the hall lined with cells on either side, perhaps wondering in their way why their friend was leaving.

"Sorry to disappoint you," I muttered, chuckling to myself. "You'll have to find another feast."

"What?" Cari looked up at me, frowning.

"Nothing."

She showed me the broken door which she'd used to get in. Likely the same door he had used.

"Wait," I said, pulling up just shy of stepping out. "What's outside? And what of me? Will I be seen like this?"

I hadn't bathed and had been living in my own filth since then. My stench embarrassed and appalled me.

"Oh. Right. I almost forgot." She bent, allowing the pack to slide from her shoulder, and pulled out fresh clothes along with two large bottles of water and a small cake of soap. "I'm sorry. This will have to do for now."

I was already halfway out of my clothes. I wished I had something to burn them with.

Minutes later, freshly dressed and somewhat cleaner, I walked out of the old prison. We were in the suburbs of Paris, the Eiffel Tower gleaming in the distance. Had it only been weeks since I stood at the top with her? And I'd thought we had problems then. What did I know?

"Gage?"

I turned to her and pulled her into my arms without a word. She buried her face against the side of my neck, shaking, her arms winding around my back and squeezing until my ribs ached. Not that it mattered.

"I'm so sorry," I whispered in her ear, holding her as tight as I could.

"You have nothing to be sorry for."

"But I do. I brought you here, to this. To him. I should've known. I was so blind about so many things."

"So was I," she insisted, clutching me. "I should've seen what he was doing. I wanted to trust him, and that was so stupid of me. You could've been free sooner than this, if I had just been smarter."

"It's all right now," I murmured, closing my eyes and willing it to be so. It was all right. I was leaving the suffering behind me. It was over.

But I did need to feed again, and soon. Instead of slaking my thirst, the blood of the hitchhiker had left me yearning for more. But at least it had left me stronger. And I was alive.

Where would I find someone to feed on? We were virtually in the middle of nowhere, miles from the city. All around the prison was open fields, and beyond that what looked like a thriving village or neighborhood. Lights twinkled there, and cars. But it wasn't the same as hunting in Paris, where a handful of nameless tourists might go unnoticed.

"I don't know that I'm strong enough to course," I mused.

"We could go over there." She pointed to the rows of homes and businesses.

"I suppose. We'd have to be careful."

"We will. You need to feed. We can move on after that. No one need know there are vampires around."

We took off on foot, cutting through the field. As we walked, we discussed our options regarding lodging.

There weren't many.

"I know this isn't something you want to hear..." she began as we drew closer to the neighborhood.

The sounds of life were strangely foreign to my ears. I had convinced myself I'd never hear the likes of it again.

"What are you thinking?"

Our hands were clasped—I thought I might never let go of her—and I squeezed to reassure her.

"The prison?"

"No. I can't do that. I don't care how safe it is. Surprising there aren't squatters and drug addicts already making it their home."

"Naomi told me there were legends about it being haunted. I wonder just how haunted it actually is, and how many of those supposed ghosts are..." She didn't have to continue.

I knew what she was trying to say. How many vampires and poor, defenseless humans had Micah locked up there over the years?

"It was enough to keep everyone away, at least," I muttered, not sure whether that was a good thing or not. I could've used the assistance, after all.

But humans might have brought more humans, and even more after that. There was such a thing as too much help.

Several restaurants were still open, and pubs. The heady

aroma of so much blood was nearly too much for me to handle without running amok.

Only Cari's hand in mine was enough to keep me grounded.

"Hey! You!"

I turned just in time to realize the angry shout was directed at me—and the angry vampire who'd shouted it was heading our way, his fists clenched.

33

GAGE

"Who is that?" Cari asked, poised for a fight. Her instincts were still strong enough that she didn't back down from a threat or even hesitate.

"I don't know." And I wasn't strong enough to fight him.

He appeared furious, eyes blazing as he marched toward us. Dark hair, short, a little spiky up top. As he drew closer, I had the feeling I might have seen him before but couldn't place the face.

"What are you doing out here?" he demanded.

"Out where?" I glanced around, confused. "Out here?"

"Who are you?" Cari asked, lifting her chin and sounding very bold and confident.

I had to give her credit.

He scoffed, looking her up and down. "What business is it of yours? What are you doing with this loser? Why don't you try telling me that?"

"Hang on, now." I stepped in between the two of them. "If you and I have business, that's fine. Don't bring her into it."

He snickered. "What, is Anissa not good enough for you now? You cross the ocean and pick up another woman in her place?"

I blinked, pulling back. "Wait. You think I'm Jonah, don't you? I'm Gage. Jonah is my twin."

It was his turn to blink and fall back a few steps. His entire body changed—his shoulders fell, fists unclenched. "Oh. Of course. I forgot there were two of you."

"You know Gage's brother?" Cari asked.

"Not personally. But by sight."

"And by Anissa," I guessed, smirking when he winced. "A friend of hers?"

"Yeah. A friend." The bitterness was thick in his voice, and I understood quickly why he appeared to hate my brother. Probably a former sweetheart, or a friend who'd always wanted to be more. The humans had a term for that which I'd heard once or twice. Friend-zone.

"What's your name?" Cari's voice was suddenly gentle. She understood, too.

"Raze. From the Carver clan."

"Ah, I see. And what's a Carver doing outside Paris? Shouldn't you be in New York?"

"I could ask the same of a Bourke," he reminded me before glancing back and forth, as though watching his back. Watching for what—or whom? "Here. Do you feel like sitting for a bit?"

"I would love nothing more."

There was an empty table at the pub in front of which we'd met up, and the three of us claimed it. There wasn't much in the way of a crowd inside or out, nor was there much foot traffic. We had enough privacy to speak at least in generalities.

He leaned in. "See, after the business with Marcus, things fell apart within the clan."

"The business with Marcus. Oh, yes. I'd heard a little bit about that."

Cari, on the other hand, seemed positively lost. I made a mental note to explain things to her later.

He nodded, frowning. "You can imagine, then. Here's the thing, many of us were already dissatisfied, well before his arrest. What he did to Anissa and Sara…" His jaw tightened, his eyes regaining the fire they'd held when he first charged at me. Yes, he felt a great deal of attachment to Anissa. Jonah couldn't like that.

He continued. "At any rate, I'd wanted to leave the clan for a long time leading up to the news that he'd been locked up. Once Marcus was imprisoned, it seemed like the natural time to make a break. I'm not the only one, though I think I'm the only one to come to Paris."

Cari's leg nudged mine, under the table. "Where are you staying? We're in need of accommodations."

"Though, if there's a strong league influence…" I began, giving him a meaningful look. I wouldn't tell him straight-out why we were running from the league until I knew I could trust him, but I couldn't allow him to lead us into the arms of the enemy, either.

He shook his head, frowning deeply. "What league? Now that Lucian's gone, there's really nothing left."

Lucian gone? I felt like I'd have to be caught up at some point. "I would beg to differ," I murmured. "The league's influence runs deep. Just because there isn't a permanent leader in place doesn't mean there aren't still those who uphold the laws set down so long ago."

"What did you do?" He looked from one of us to the other. "Why are you hiding from them?"

"Who said we're hiding?" Cari asked.

She would've made a decent professional gambler, with a poker face like hers.

"Why else did you come all the way out here?"

I leaned forward. "I could ask you the same thing, then. It seems a long way to run simply out of dissatisfaction."

"Sometimes, you want to put an ocean between yourself and others," he replied, and I understood.

No wonder he'd been furious when he mistook me for Jonah. He'd come all this way to forget him and Anissa.

His smile was tight. "But don't worry, no matter why you want to avoid them. There's no connection to the league. I fell in with a rather ragtag group of outsiders. Genevieve was no picnic, from what I understand. This band fled her leadership decades ago and set up their own arrangement. Like a commune of sorts. They flew under her radar for a long time."

I weighed our options. We could either survive on the streets, scrambling to find shelter every morning and murdering in the evening—we'd have to move on quickly, before it became clear we were spreading death wherever we went—or we could take a chance on Raze and his group of outsiders.

I had no idea there were so many. It made me wonder how many there could've been back in the States.

Cari watched me, waiting for my decision. I knew she'd follow whatever course of action I set us on. Not only was she a babe in the woods when it came to clan business, but she trusted me. Even after I'd led us to near destruction in Paris, she trusted my judgment. I wanted nothing more than to prove myself worthy of that trust.

"We're searching for someplace to stay," I reasoned. "And

I'm in great need of something..." We exchanged another meaningful look.

"They have a bank in place," he assured me. "Synthetic, but better than some alternatives."

"Believe me." Cari and I glanced at each other. "Anything's better than some alternatives." I remembered the rats, a chill running down my spine. Perhaps not anything...

"By all means, let's get moving. It's not far, maybe fifteen minutes. You seem rather worn. Are you sure you can make it?"

"You just lead the way," I assured him with a grim smile.

Cari took my arm as the three of us set out. "Do you get the feeling we're always jumping out of a burning building and into whatever looks slightly less threatening?"

I chuckled, kissing the top of her head with greater humor than I actually felt. Yes, I had that exact feeling. Living without actual choices wasn't something I was accustomed to. We had no other option but to take advantage of what speared to be a stroke of good luck in meeting up with Raze.

The only question was, would it turn out to be such good luck? We wouldn't know until we arrived.

"Did I forget to thank you?" I murmured.

"You don't have to thank me." She tilted her head up so our eyes met, and I remembered the time we met. And the second, as well. How she'd captivated me from the first minute as we'd walked through Manhattan. Now, we were outside Paris, and our situation was greatly changed.

But she was still captivating. I was still in her thrall, just as much as ever—especially after she'd saved me from a living hell.

"Even so. Thank you."

"Now, we're even," she reasoned, smiling as she wrapped

her arms around mine and leaned her head on my shoulder. "Or at least, closer to even." To the average passerby, we were a loving couple walking with a friend, enjoying an evening together.

They didn't know we were escaping an unspeakably horrific past and walking into an uncertain future.

At least I had her at my side.

I hope you enjoyed *Vindication*! I can't wait to bring you the next book in this series!

Sign up for the newsletter to be notified when it's released.

For Rye's website put the following in a browser:
www.leagueofvampires.com
To sign up for the newsletter put this in a browser:
mailerlite.com/webforms/landing/k9z2k8

Made in United States
Orlando, FL
06 February 2022